Warfare
in the
RENAISSANCE WORLD

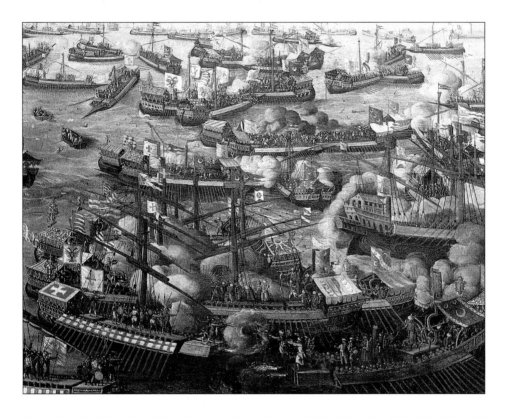

HISTORY OF WARFARE

Paul Brewer

RSVP
RAINTREE
STECK-VAUGHN
PUBLISHERS
A Steck-Vaughn Company

Steck-Vaughn Company

First published 1999 by Raintree Steck-Vaughn Publishers,
an imprint of Steck-Vaughn Company.
Copyright © 1999 Brown Partworks Limited.

Library of Congress Cataloging-in-Publication Data

Brewer, Paul.
   Warfare in the Renaissance world / Paul Brewer.
      p.   cm. — (History of warfare)
   Includes bibliographical references and index.
   Summary: Describes the widespread changes in the conduct of war that occurred in the 200 years between the beginning of the sixteenth century and the end of the seventeenth century.
   ISBN 0-8172-5444-7
   1. Military history, Modern — 16th century — Juvenile literature.
   2. Military history, Modern — 17th century — Juvenile literature.
   3. Military art and science — History — 16th century — Juvenile literature.   4. Military art and science — History — 17th century — Juvenile literature.   [1. Military history , Modern — 16th century.
   2. Military history, Modern — 17th century.   3. Military art and science — History — 16th century.   Military art and science — History — 17th century.]   I. Series: History of warfare (Austin, Tex.)
   U39.B74   1999
   355'.009'031 — dc21   98-3388
                                                                  CIP
                                                                  AC

Printed and bound in the United States
1 2 3 4 5 6 7 8 9 0 IP 03 02 01 00 99 98

Brown Partworks Limited
Managing Editor: Ian Westwell
Senior Designer: Paul Griffin
Picture Researcher: Wendy Verren
Editorial Assistant: Antony Shaw
Cartographers: William le Bihan, John See
Index: Pat Coward

Front cover: The Ottomans besiege Vienna in 1683 (main picture) and King Gustavus Adolphus of Sweden (inset).
Page 1: The Battle of Lepanto between Christian and Turkish fleets, 1571.

Raintree Steck-Vaughn
Publishing Director: Walter Kossmann
Project Manager: Joyce Spicer
Editor: Shirley Shalit

Consultant
Dr. Niall Barr, Senior Lecturer,
Royal Military Academy Sandhurst,
Camberley, Surrey, England

Acknowledgments listed on page 80 constitute part of this copyright page.

CONTENTS

INTRODUCTION

This volume of History of Warfare looks at the widespread changes in technology and the conduct of war that occurred between the beginning of the 16th century and the end of the 17th century, a period known to historians as the Renaissance. By the late 1600s wars had became usually longer, generals were more skilled—although they remained members of the nobility or upper classes—and soldiers were professionals who received pay and training. The increasingly dominant weapons on land were early muskets and mobile artillery.

These changes were gradual. Pikes, for example, had been around for many centuries but continued in ever-decreasing use until the end of the 17th century as the infantryman's chief defense against cavalry. They finally disappeared when infantry began to be equipped with the bayonet, a weapon that could be used to beat off a cavalry attack. Muskets themselves became more reliable and were increasingly cheap due to mass production. New recruits enlisted in (or were forced into) standing, regular units varying in strength from approximately 500 to 1,000 men. These standing regiments often encouraged better morale and personal pride among the ordinary soldiers, whose brightly colored uniforms often indicated their membership in a particular unit.

Artillery also became a key weapon. Cannon were of three main types. The culverin was a heavy weapon able to fire large cannonballs accurately over relatively long distances with a flat trajectory, or path. The howitzer was a lighter weapon used to fire at targets hidden behind hills. It had a

curved, plunging trajectory. The mortar was used against fortifications. It had a short range and a very high trajectory.

Cavalry still charged across battlefields, but gradually lost their armor as it offered little protection against musket fire. Cavalrymen still used swords, but new types began to be equipped with pistols and short muskets. These troops raided enemy supply lines, gathered information on enemy activity or territory, or fought on foot once they were in action.

Armies were becoming larger as countries became rich enough to support them both in times of war and peace. They also received better support. They were accompanied by supply trains carrying food for men and animals and extra ammunition. However, most armies needed to be resupplied on a regular basis. Towns and cities were turned into supply bases and heavily fortified. By the late 17th century wars often centered around the defense or capture of these fortresses. The supremacy of artillery forced a major rethink in siege warfare by attackers and defenders alike.

Warfare at sea also underwent huge changes. Ship and cannon designs were transformed. Warships were able to brave the high seas, operating many hundreds of miles from their home ports. Naval battles were no longer decided in hand-to-hand combat, but by artillery fire. Cannon were mounted along the sides of warships and captains used their fire to smash enemy vessels at long range. These new warships, weapons, and tactics meant that navies were no longer used solely to support land operations. Warships could fight and win wars on their own.

FRANCE AND SPAIN'S WARS IN ITALY

 King Charles VIII of France was a relation of the family that had once ruled Naples in the south of Italy. In 1494 he decided to reclaim the throne of Naples and invaded Italy. The great strength of his army was its artillery. In the past guns were mounted on carts that were hard to move or on platforms that had no wheels. Because their barrels were made of iron, they were also very heavy. Charles, however, had much lighter bronze guns and wheeled gun carriers. Gunpowder weapons were becoming decisive.

Charles's campaign in Italy against Naples began a new era in warfare—one based on firepower and professional (often mercenary) infantry. The previously humble foot soldier was becoming much more important than his country's nobles in battle. Armed with either early firearms and pikes (the pikes protected the troops with firearms, who could only fire once or twice a minute and had no bayonet at the time, from cavalry attack), infantry backed by artillery were able to defeat cavalry. Cavalrymen began to give up armor to save weight and increase their mobility.

Charles VIII of France makes a triumphant entry into the Italian city of Florence in 1494. He had already captured Naples. Other European states were so worried about his growing power that they formed an alliance against him.

At the end of the 15th century Italy was the richest region of Europe. But it did not owe its wealth to political stability or unity. It was divided up into many states usually ruled over by the government of a single city. Some of these states, like Milan or Naples, were large. Others, like Venice and Florence, were rich. Smaller states, like Savoy and Siena, survived because a more powerful state supported them against their larger neighbors. Many of the Italian states, both large and small, sought the support of more powerful kingdoms outside Italy for help against

GERMAN LANDSKNECHTS

In 1486 the Holy Roman Emperor Maximilian built up a permanent army. The infantrymen were known as landsknechts, a name meaning "land knights" that was usually applied to all the German mercenaries who copied the colorful uniforms of these troops.

The landsknechts considered themselves a special society of soldiers. They recruited by sending a drummer and a man waving a banner through the streets. Those who wished to join up fell in behind the two and marched to the landsknecht camp. They entered through a kind of gate formed by a pike laid across the top of two poles, then formed a circle and gave an oath of loyalty to obey the rules of the landsknechts.

Ordinary people, such as bakers and shoemakers, joined the landsknechts because mercenary service gave them the chance to make a fortune through looting. The landsknechts were generally excellent soldiers, certainly better than the poorly trained troops they usually faced on the field of battle. Only the Swiss and, later, the Spanish had infantry units equal to those of the landsknechts.

Landsknechts dressed in their multicolored costumes. German landsknechts and Swiss infantry were the best foot soldiers in Europe during the late 15th and early 16th centuries.

FRANCE AND SPAIN AT WAR IN ITALY

Italy was made up of several kingdoms and was the site of a long series of wars between France and Spain and their Italian allies. Both France and Spain's royal families had rival claims to Italy.

their neighbors. Milan and Florence, for example, allowed Charles VIII to march through their territories because they wanted him to help them in their own ambitions.

The family that actually ruled Naples in 1494 was related to the Spanish royal family. When Charles took Naples, the Spanish helped form an anti-French alliance. The Holy Roman emperor, the pope, Venice, and Milan agreed to join. The Holy Roman emperor was head of a federation of states in central Europe stretching from what is now Denmark to northern Italy. Spain sent an army to Italy. Faced with such a powerful alliance, Charles decided to march back to France in 1495. On the way he defeated an alliance army at Fornovo in July. In October Milan came to a peace agreement with Charles.

The invasion by Charles VIII was the first in a series of wars between France and Spain in Italy. Constantly shifting allegiances

7

SPAIN'S MILITARY SYSTEM

The Spanish infantry companies that arrived in Italy in 1495 consisted of a mixture of about 200 soldiers armed with either pikes, halberds (axes mounted on short poles), or swords and shields, crossbows, or harquebuses (early firearms). The commander of the army, Gonzalo Fernandez de Cordoba, grouped three of these companies together to form larger units.

In 1505 the Spanish king made this arrangement official when he established larger units called colunelas (columns) of five companies. As armies got bigger during the 16th century, the colunelas began to be grouped together. The most important cause was the Spanish discovery of the powerful effect of massed shooting from harquebuses on enemy attacks. Pikes were used to stop cavalry charges or in hand-to-hand combat.

During the 1530s it became usual for three colunelas to be combined into a tercio. By this time companies were made up entirely of soldiers armed with pikes or firearms. The tercio system lasted until the late 17th century and was the first attempt to organize troops on a permanent regimental system.

make it a confusing story. The true character of these wars was revealed in 1500, when King Louis XII of France and King Ferdinand of Spain agreed to divide up the state of Naples between them. What happened there was repeated across Italy.

The best general of the age

The French occupied Naples in 1501 but refused to hand over to Ferdinand his share. In March 1502 a fleet of Spanish galleys landed an army at Taranto commanded by Gonzalo Fernandez de Cordoba. Cordoba was probably one of the best generals of the age. He led a brilliant campaign that drove the French out of Naples. At the Battle of Cerignola on April 28, 1503, he put his firearm-carrying infantry behind a palisade (wooden fence). Their steady firing killed many of the attacking French and their Swiss mercenaries. It was the first battle in European history won solely by gunpowder weapons.

On December 29, 1503, Cordoba planned a quick surprise crossing of the Garigliano River. His engineers used the cover of bad weather to secretly build a bridge across the swollen river. His forces then swarmed across the bridge and stormed the French camp. French casualties were heavy. In 1505 Louis XII gave up the French claim to Naples.

France and Spain went to war again in Italy in 1510, when Pope Julius II formed an alliance known as the Holy League to oppose French ambitions in Italy. The battleground now shifted to northern Italy, where the armies of Louis XII had taken over Milan in 1499. In 1512 a French army invaded the Papal state, the lands ruled by the pope in Italy.

The Battle of Ravenna was fought on April 11 between the French and a Spanish-Papal army. Ravenna is generally regarded as the dividing line between medieval and renaissance warfare.

The French general, Gaston de Foix, sent an invitation to a battle with the Spanish commander, Raymond de Cardona. Despite these knightly courtesies the fighting was most unchivalrous. A long bombardment was followed by a ferocious hand-to-hand fight between the infantry of both sides in the Spanish trenches. The French won but de Foix was killed. The French suffered 4,500 casualties, the Spanish-Papal army some 9,000.

French victory at Marignano

The war ended in March 1514. During the previous four months different members of the Holy League had individually signed peace treaties with France. The last was the Holy Roman emperor. The peace lasted for just 14 months. In June 1515 the new

King Francis I of France (center) leads a cavalry charge against Swiss pikemen during the Battle of Marignano in September 1515. Francis won the battle and the Italian-Swiss alliance ranged against him collapsed.

French king, Francis I, allied with the Italian city-state of Venice and attacked other Italian city-states. One of these, Milan, had been taken over by the Swiss and Francis wanted it. The French won the war after the Battle of Marignano against the Swiss.

The Swiss countered the French advantage in guns at Marignano by attacking rapidly. Neither side could break the other in fighting on the first day. On the second day fighting resumed but the Swiss withdrew when they learned of the approach of a Venetian army. By December 1516 French control over Milan was recognized throughout Western Europe.

Peace might have lasted some time had not the ruler of Spain and the Netherlands, Charles I, been elected Holy Roman emperor in 1519, becoming Charles V. He now controlled almost all the territory running along France's borders. Charles and Francis I of France were to fight four wars, largely in Italy, during the next 25 years.

New gunpowder weapons

The first war, between 1521 and 1526, revealed the dominance of gunpowder weapons. In the Battle of Bicocca on April 27, 1522, a French army with Swiss mercenaries attacked a Spanish-German-Papal one. The Swiss, whose skill with the pike was legendary, attempted to storm an entrenched position. The French commander had wanted to delay the attack until his artillery was

The Battle of Pavia was fought on February 24, 1525, and saw the cream of France's mounted nobility smashed by Spanish infantry armed with early muskets. Here, badly mauled French cavalry retreat in disorder after a failed charge against the steady Spanish infantry.

THE BATTLE OF PAVIA

At the end of January 1525 the French army in Italy, commanded in person by King Francis I, was besieging the town of Pavia. Francis had about 25,000 troops. He learned that an army of 20,000, commanded by the Spanish general Fernando Francisco de Avalos, was advancing to help the garrison of Pavia.

On the night of February 24 de Avalos's army broke camp and marched around the left flank of the French force. When the sun rose, Francis realized that his position was in danger. He took his heavy cavalry force and attacked immediately to buy time for the rest of his army to face in the new direction.

While his charge halted the enemy advance, it did not give the rest of the French army time to prepare. When the enemy resumed their attack, the garrison of Pavia also came out to attack the French siege works. Caught between two attacks most of the French infantry retreated. Francis was captured.

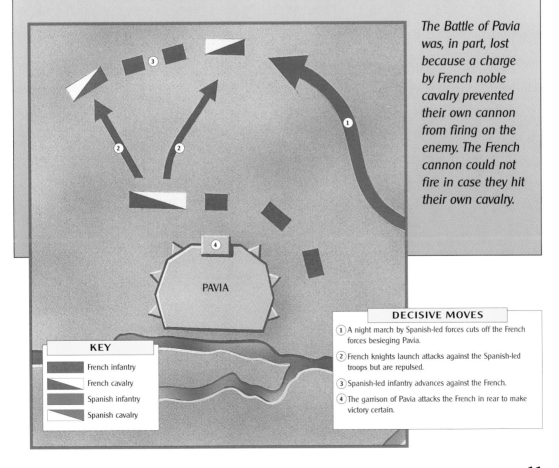

The Battle of Pavia was, in part, lost because a charge by French noble cavalry prevented their own cannon from firing on the enemy. The French cannon could not fire in case they hit their own cavalry.

PAVIA

KEY

	French infantry
	French cavalry
	Spanish infantry
	Spanish cavalry

DECISIVE MOVES

1. A night march by Spanish-led forces cuts off the French forces besieging Pavia.

2. French knights launch attacks against the Spanish-led troops but are repulsed.

3. Spanish-led infantry advances against the French.

4. The garrison of Pavia attacks the French in rear to make victory certain.

in position. The Swiss refused to wait. They were shot to pieces by Spanish gunfire. Some 3,000 were killed in 30 minutes. The supremacy of the Swiss infantry was over.

The Battle of Pavia on February 24, 1525, showed that the age of the mounted knight was also drawing to a close. King Francis repeatedly charged the Spanish harquebusiers with his lance-armed armored knights. Each attack was beaten off with heavy casualties. In the end Francis's own horse was shot dead; he was wounded and captured. It was a humiliating defeat. Most of the 8,000 French losses were due to gunfire.

The most symbolic incident of the new age came between these two battles. Twenty years earlier a Spanish army took refuge in the port of Barletta in the kingdom of Naples. A French army besieged it there. The aristocrats of both sides engaged in knightly jousts with one another to pass the time. The most successful French champion was a knight called Bayard. On April 30, 1524, Bayard was killed at the Battle of the Sesia River in northern Italy. He was leading a cavalry charge like a knight of old when he was shot dead by a "lowly" harquebusier.

The peace that ended this first war lasted four months. Francis had arranged it while a captive in Madrid. As soon as he was released, he formed an alliance against Charles. It included those Italian rulers who a decade before had been allied against France. The war that followed showed the changes in warfare that had been brought about by the last war's battles.

The importance of fortresses

Armies now maneuvered to capture fortresses, instead of seeking out one another to fight. Improvements to fortifications, especially in digging earthworks on the battlefield, had provided a successful counterbalance to the mobility of field artillery. A march through Italy like that by Charles VIII of France in 1494 was, by 1528, impossible to copy. When the French tried it that year, only 5,000 survived out of an army of 30,000.

The one notable event of the second war was the sack of Rome by the army of Charles V in 1527. Its savagery stunned all Europe. After the war Charles V made sure almost all Italy was either ruled directly by him or by a family allied to him. Only Venice and the pope had any kind of independence.

The last two wars between Charles and Francis, between 1536 and 1538 and 1542 and 1544 changed nothing. Most of the fighting took place on France's northern and western frontiers, showing Spain's unshakable control over Italy. The last major war between France and Spain occurred between 1552 and 1559. The French first seized the frontier fortresses of Metz, Verdun, and Toul, then waited for the enemy's counterattack. Charles led an army to Metz but the three-month siege of the fortress ended in failure in January 1553.

By the time the war ended Charles had abdicated (retired from ruling), giving Spain and Italy to his son Philip II, and his Austrian lands to his brother Ferdinand. France had abandoned Italy to Spain, but had made important gains in the north and west. France and Spain, however, would be at war again.

Charles I of Spain (who later also became the Holy Roman emperor and took the title Charles V) fought a number of wars against the French for control of Italy and parts of Western Europe. Eventually wearied by the long wars, Charles abdicated in October 1556, dividing his lands between his son and brother.

FRANCE'S WARS OF RELIGION

The death of Francis II of France in 1560 put his ten-year-old brother on the throne as Charles IX. The boy's mother, Catherine de Medici, and an important noble, Francis, Duke of Guise, ruled the country as Charles was so young. Both were devout Catholics. They opposed the spread of the Protestant faith in France. Many of France's leading Protestant nobles, such as Louis, Prince of Condé, believed that they could gain control of the government and protect the followers of their faith from persecution. Civil war was inevitable.

Protestants tried to assassinate Guise early in 1562. On March 1 enraged Catholics in Vassy, a town in eastern France, massacred its Protestant inhabitants. In April Condé and the Lord High Admiral, Gaspard de Coligny, another Protestant noble, called for a national uprising of French Protestants, who were known as Huguenots. They seized the city of Orléans and fighting broke out across the country. Atrocities and massacres were committed by both sides and became widespread.

The Battle of Dreux was fought on December 19, 1562, and ended in a narrow Catholic victory. This engraving of the battle shows cavalry attacking musketeers and pikemen in a defensive square (top left) and cavalry using pistols to stop an enemy cavalry charge (center, left).

GERMAN CAVALRY

The French Huguenots received aid from Protestants in Germany. This included mercenary heavy cavalry known as reiters, the German word for rider. These troops used a firearm that could be held in a single hand. This pistol had been invented in Germany in about 1517.

The pistol used a mechanism known as the wheel lock. A spring connected to a small wheel was wound tightly using a key. Pulling the trigger caused the spring to lose its tension, and the wheel to spin against a flint. The sparks thrown up by this action ignited powder in the firing pan, firing the gun.

This weapon was used in a formation known as the caracole. The reiters charged at a trot. When the front rank was near enough, the riders fired, then turned to the side to allow the following rank to shoot.

Pages from a 15th-century training manual showing the correct procedures for firing a wheel lock pistol.

Protestant strength was concentrated in the outer regions of France. Catholic France's strength lay around Paris, the capital, and in Burgundy to the east. Protestants were generally stronger in the provincial towns and Catholics in the countryside. The Protestants also received help from England's Protestant monarch, Queen Elizabeth I.

The English sent an expedition to capture the Catholic-held Channel port of Le Havre. The Huguenots also sent an army to besiege Le Havre. While marching from Orléans to Le Havre, the Huguenots bumped into a Catholic army that had come from successfully besieging the city of Rouen, and was intending to attack Orléans. Battle between the two was inevitable.

Casualties were heavy, about 4,000 for each side, in the Battle of Dreux on December 19, 1562. Both of the rival commanders—the Protestant Condé and the Catholic Duke Anne of Montmorency—were captured. The Catholic army, now with Francis Guise in command, was able to continue to Orléans and lay siege to the city. When Francis, Duke of Guise, was assassinated, Catherine de Medici got both sides to negotiate a peace settlement. The French Catholics and Protestants united to besiege Le Havre, forcing the English to surrender in July 1563.

The uneasy peace lasted five years, until some Huguenot nobles, led by the released Condé and Coligny, attempted to kidnap the French royal family. A Huguenot army failed to seize Paris. Because the Huguenots were scattered so widely around the country, the Catholics could not defeat them. If the Catholics were victorious in one part of the country, the Huguenots often assembled a new army elsewhere.

Mercenary atrocities

Condé was murdered in March 1569 after he was captured at the Battle of Jarnac. Coligny, however, kept the war going by laying siege to Poitiers. A Catholic army raised the siege and then defeated Coligny and his army at Moncontour on October 3. Both sides were evenly matched and made use of mercenaries. The Swiss used by the Catholics took considerable delight in slaughtering the Huguenot German mercenaries. Some 8,000 Huguenots perished while Catholic losses were around 1,000. The way was open for the Catholic army to take La Rochelle, a port vital to the Huguenot cause. Instead the army laid siege to nearby Saint-Jean d'Angely. The Huguenots were given time to create a new army in the southwest of the country.

In 1570 Coligny launched his army across central France. As he approached Paris, Catherine de Medici convinced Charles IX to negotiate a peace settlement. Coligny had brought Henry of Navarre, a Protestant relative of the French royal family, along with him on his last campaigns. The Huguenots arranged his marriage to Margaret, a sister of Charles IX.

Thousands of Protestants gathered in Paris to celebrate the marriage in 1572. This was convenient for Catherine de Medici, who was still plotting against the Protestants. On the night of August 23–24, Catholic soldiers butchered thousands of Protestants in the streets. Among the victims was Coligny. The St. Bartholomew's Eve massacre stunned Protestants throughout Europe but also shocked many French Catholics.

Having killed many leading Huguenots, the Catholics attacked La Rochelle, where Huguenot supplies arrived from Protestants abroad. The siege dragged on into the summer of 1573. Some 20,000 Catholic soldiers were killed or wounded.

A new group emerged in French politics—Catholics who were tired of the Guise family's hatred of Protestantism. After the death of Charles IX in 1574, the leader of this group was crowned King Henry III. In 1576 he negotiated the Peace of Beaulieu with the Huguenots.

The murder of thousands of French Protestants by Catholics on St. Bartholomew's Eve in 1572.

Henry, Duke of Guise, son of Duke Francis, rejected the peace. With support from Catholic Spain, he prepared to begin a new war against the Huguenots. He organized the Holy League to defend Catholic interests. Under its influence Henry III decreed an end to religious tolerance in 1585. All Huguenot France now rebelled under the leadership of Henry of Navarre, one of the leading Huguenots. Navarre was a region of France.

Henry of Navarre proved to be a remarkable general. He defeated a Holy League army at Coutras in southwest France in October 1587. His musketeers blasted the Catholic cavalry and his cavalry swept them from the field. The Huguenot infantry and cavalry then combined to smash the Catholic infantry.

The following year Henry, Duke of Guise, ordered soldiers of the Holy League to seize Paris. King Henry III briefly became a puppet of the League, but plotted against its leadership. Henry Guise and his brother Louis were murdered in December 1588. However, in August 1589 Henry III was assassinated by a monk.

Henry of Navarre (center) leads a charge of Protestant cavalry at the Battle of Ivry on March 14, 1590. His attack routed the Catholics, except for their Swiss mercenaries who fought on until they agreed to favorable surrender terms.

ALESSANDRO FARNESE, DUKE OF PARMA

Catholic Spain's commander in the Netherlands (then a Spanish possession) from 1578 to 1592, Alessandro Farnese, Duke of Parma, was probably the greatest general in Europe at the end of the 16th century. He was a nephew of King Philip II of Spain, and was raised at the Spanish court. He arrived in the Netherlands in 1577 as an assistant to the viceroy, Don Juan of Austria. At the time Dutch Protestants were rebelling against their Spanish overlords. The Dutch wanted their own country and freedom of worship.

After Don Juan died in October 1578 Philip II appointed Parma viceroy. By 1587 he had restored a large part of the area to Spanish rule. Had he not been ordered by Philip to prepare for a great invasion of England in 1588 and then to invade France in 1590, Parma might well have defeated the Dutch rebellion. As it was he died at Arras in December 1592.

Alessandro Farnese, although born in Italy, was a loyal servant of Spain and was a master of outmaneuvering his opponents before offering battle.

Henry of Navarre was now legitimately king of France. He became Henry IV. The Holy League refused to accept this. However, in two battles in northern France—at Arques in 1589 and Ivry in 1590—he defeated the Holy League's main field armies. He next laid siege to Paris. King Philip II of Spain now ordered his commander in the Netherlands, Alessandro Farnese, Duke of Parma, to invade France in support of the League. Parma advanced on Paris, forcing Henry of Navarre to raise the siege. The next two years saw Henry and Parma engage in a war of maneuver. Neither gained any permanent advantage.

Henry eventually renounced his Protestant faith and become a Catholic. This was in July 1593 and he entered Paris in March 1594. The Edict of Nantes, issued by Henry in 1598, guaranteed religious freedom in France and brought the wars to an end.

19

THE OTTOMAN EMPIRE

After ending a war with Venice in 1503, the Ottoman Turks paused in their attempts to expand their empire deeper into Europe and the Middle East. The Ottoman ruler, Sultan Bayazid II, regarded such wars as too costly and risky. However, his sons, especially Selim, had a different view. When Selim emerged the winner in a civil war with his brothers that lasted from 1509 to 1512, he forced his father to give up the throne. Selim became sultan. He began to look for new conquests in the Middle East and Christian Europe.

Selim first turned against Persia, which had supported one of his brothers during the civil war. Victory at the Battle of Chaldiran in August 1515 enabled his army to capture the Persian capital, Tabriz, in September. However, his army mutinied, refusing to advance any farther into Persia. This allowed the Persian ruler, Shah Ismail, to recover his capital.

The Egyptians routed

Selim gathered his army again the next year but learned that both of the Ottomans' neighbors, Persia and Egypt, had allied to invade Turkey. Selim moved his army south to Syria, where the Egyptian forces were gathering. The two armies clashed at Merj-Dabik. The Egyptian cavalry charged the Turkish positions but the Turks had plenty of artillery and harquebusiers to deal with the cavalry. The gunfire killed many of the Egyptians, including their commander, and they were quickly routed.

The victory at Merj-Dabik enabled the Turks to occupy Syria. They continued their advance south. In January 1517 at the Battle of Ridanieh the Egyptians showed they had learned some lessons. Sixteenth-century field guns were heavy and hard to move on the battlefield so the Egyptians decided to wait for a Turkish attack. The Turkish artillery would be less effective at long range. However, the Turks simply bombarded the Egyptians at long range. As more and more Egyptians were killed or wounded, they

An Ottoman cavalryman of the 16th century. He is protected by a mixture of plate and chain-mail armor and carries a lance.

chose to attack rather than suffer further losses. Their charge failed, as it had at Merj-Dabik. This victory allowed Selim to conquer Egypt and add it to his empire.

War against Christian Europe

Selim's empire was now the strongest in the Islamic world of the Middle East and Mediterranean. Other rulers turned to him for help. The Christians of Spain threatened the religious Islamic ruler of Algiers, Khair-ed-Din. He sent word to Selim that he would acknowledge the sultan as his overlord if, in turn, Selim would protect Algiers from the Spaniards. Since the Algerians had a powerful fleet that would be of great use to the Ottomans in later campaigns in the Mediterranean, Selim was happy to agree.

Having secured his eastern and southern frontiers Selim now turned back to Europe. However, as he prepared to attack the island of Rhodes, then in Christian hands, he died. Christendom may have felt safe but it was much too soon. Selim's successor, Suleiman the Magnificent, spent most of his reign waging war against Christian Europe.

The Knights of St. John

Suleiman began with an offensive in 1521 that captured Belgrade. Then, in June 1522, he attacked Rhodes, the small fortress island belonging to the Order of the Knights of St. John of Jerusalem. Suleiman mobilized an army of 100,000 to send against the 700 knights and their 6,000 Rhodian soldiers. It took six months of hard fighting for Suleiman to take the island. He allowed the Christian forces to evacuate Rhodes. Only 180 knights and 1,500 other soldiers were left alive, most were wounded. They settled on Malta in 1530. The island was a gift to them from the Holy Roman Emperor Charles V.

THE JANISSARIES

The backbone of the Turkish army rested in a powerful corps of infantry known as the Janissaries ("new soldiers"). They were founded in 1362 and were first raised from Christian prisoners of war.

From the 15th century onward Christian communities under Ottoman rule were required to supply a number of their young men each year to serve in the corps of Janissaries. The youngsters converted to Islam and became the personal property of the sultan. This disciplined infantry was often the edge that the Turkish army needed to defeat enemies that lacked this element in their armies.

Unlike the other elements of the Turkish army, such as the spahi (soldier) cavalry, the akinji (scout) cavalry, and the azab (young and unmarried) infantry, the Janissaries were kept permanently under arms.

The corps was divided into a number of separate companies. There were about 200 in the 1580s. The Aga (leader) of the Janissaries commanded the whole corps. Each Janissary company contained between 100 and 500 men and had a distinctive uniform.

An aerial view of Vienna during the Ottoman siege of 1529. Vienna was defended by 17,000 troops. The Ottomans tried to capture the great city from September to October, but could not break in. With the onset of colder weather the Ottomans withdrew, but not before beheading all of their Christian prisoners.

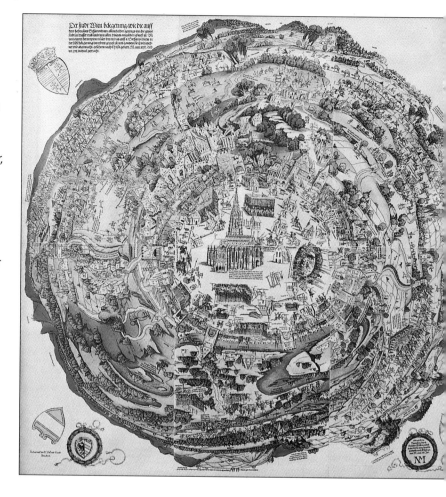

Suleiman now turned north again and attacked Hungary in 1526. He destroyed the Hungarian army at the Battle of Mohacs in that year. In 1529 he attacked Austria and laid siege to its capital, Vienna. It was a difficult siege as the Austrians had organized their defenses well. Suleiman decided to end the siege rather than continue it through the winter. This setback delayed a further attack for three years. The invasion of 1532 also ended in failure.

The war at sea

Turkey now faced enemies in all directions. The Persians invaded the east of the empire, while Charles V, who was also king of Spain, used the Spanish fleet to raid the Peloponnese in Greece. Suleiman's alliance with Khair-ed-Din provided the naval forces he needed to counter the Christians in the Mediterranean, while he turned east with his army. Success in the east, however, was balanced by defeats in the Mediterranean. Charles V captured Tunis in 1535, defeating Khair-ed-Din's fleet during the campaign. A Turkish attempt to capture Corfu, an island held by the Venetians, failed in 1537 due to the timely arrival of a Christian fleet.

The tide only began to turn in 1538, when Khair-ed-Din out-maneuvered the Christian fleet commanded by Andrea Doria off Preveza on the west coast of Greece. Andrea Doria retreated rather than fight on unfavorable terms. A major Christian fleet did not return to this part of the world for 35 years.

Three years later Charles V tried to capture Algiers. A terrible storm destroyed his fleet and he had to withdraw. Khair-ed-Din was able to bring a fleet to the western Mediterranean and terrorize the coasts of Spain and Italy. For the next 20 years the Turks waged a naval war against Christian Europe. This only ended in 1565, when Suleiman sent another expedition against the Knights of St. John, who had constructed a new fortress on

The Ottoman Empire during the late 16th century. Successful wars had spread the empire's influence throughout the Middle East and deep into Eastern Europe.

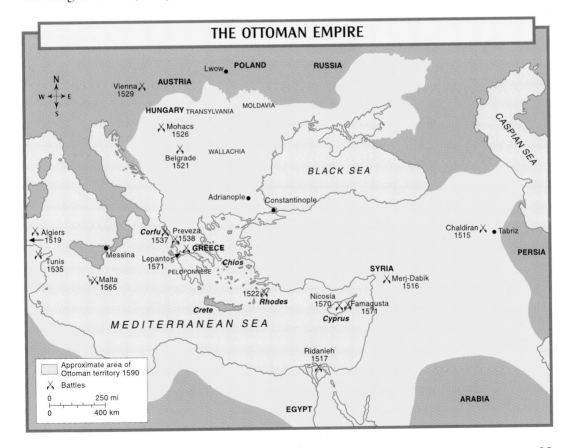

THE OTTOMAN EMPIRE

Malta. Suleiman's expeditionary force, however, was defeated by the brave defense of the island by the knights. The 60,000 Turks, backed by heavy artillery, pounded the fortress and tried to storm its walls. The valiant defenders, about 600 knights and 9,000 soldiers, resisted every attack. When a Christian relief force arrived, the Turks withdrew, leaving behind 24,000 dead.

The limits of power

Suleiman died the following year. During his reign the Ottoman Empire reached the peak of its power. His son, Selim II, wanted to consolidate Turkish power in the eastern Mediterranean. In 1570 the Turks attacked Cyprus, an island then ruled by Venice. The two main fortresses fell after sieges. The Turks stormed the walls of Nicosia on September 9, 1570, while Famagusta surrendered on August 3, 1571. At Famagusta, the leaders of the garrison were murdered by the Ottomans after surrendering.

The land and naval forces of Charles V attack Tunis, the Tunisian capital, in 1535. Charles captured the city and put in place a ruler willing to support the Christians against the Ottoman Empire.

The pope, Pius V, in response to the outbreak of war between Venice and Turkey, formed the Holy League to conduct a crusade against the Turks. The league assembled a fleet at Messina, Sicily, commanded by Don Juan of Austria. In October 1571 it defeated the Turkish fleet at the Battle of Lepanto. In 1574 Selim II died, and another weak ruler, Murad III, became sultan.

War with Persia began again in 1577. The Turks invaded Persia but were unable to achieve a lasting victory. The Holy Roman emperor, Rudolf, took advantage of the conflict in 1590 to break a cease-fire that the two great empires, Ottoman Turkey and the Holy Roman Empire, had signed in 1568.

Jean de la Valette, (center), the grand master of the Knights of St. John, gives thanks for the arrival of the Spanish fleet that forced the Ottomans to abandon their siege of Malta in September 1565.

Ottoman troops mutiny

Murad made peace with Persia and attacked westward. The war between the Hapsburg rulers of the Holy Roman Empire and the Ottomans lasted until 1606. The Hapsburgs were a Christian ruling family dynasty, which controlled the Holy Roman Empire of central Europe. The fighting largely took place in Hungary. The first big battles occurred there in 1593, when the Hapsburg army invaded and crushed the Turkish local forces in June.

The main Turkish army attempted to advance on Vienna in the autumn of that year. The Ottomans' elite Janissaries mutinied rather than start a long siege close to winter. In 1594 the Turkish attack was held up by unexpectedly tough resistance at a fortress on the Danube River. The following year Christian subjects in the provinces of Transylvania, Wallachia, and Moldavia rebelled, and Turkish forces in Hungary were defeated by a Hapsburg army.

Victory at Kerestes

However, Murad died that year and his successor, Mohammed III, scored important successes in his campaign in Hungary in 1596. The Hapsburg army attempted to halt the Turkish advance

THE BATTLE OF LEPANTO

The Battle of Lepanto on October 7, 1571, decisively altered the balance of naval forces in the Mediterranean between Christian Europe and the Turks.

The Christian fleet, commanded by Don Juan of Austria, met the Turkish fleet, commanded by Ali Monizindade, off the mouth of the Gulf of Corinth. There was no attempt to maneuver. Both fleets simply lined up and rowed toward one another.

The Christian fleet numbered 250 ships, the Turks' 270. The Christian galleys had more guns mounted and their soldiers had more harquebuses. The Christian fleet also included six Venetian galleasses, large galleys that carried extra cannon but moved much more slowly.

A combination of the galleasses and the superior numbers of Christian guns won the battle for Don Juan. Some 15,000 Turkish sailors and soldiers died, and the Turks had 53 galleys sunk and 117 captured. The Christians lost 13 warships and 7,500 dead. Over 15,000 Christian slaves used to pull the oars of Turkish warships were rescued but around 10,000 more may have drowned chained to their oars in sinking ships. Among the 8,000 Christian wounded was Miguel Cervantes, Spanish author of the book *Don Quixote*. He lost his left hand in the battle.

Christian and Ottoman warships clash at Lepanto. Superior firepower and seamanship gave the Christians a decisive edge in the battle.

at the Battle of Kerestes in October 1596. The fighting lasted three days. The Turks emerged victorious thanks to a surprise attack by Turkish cavalry on the rear of the Hapsburg positions. The crisis of the Ottoman Empire in Europe passed.

The war between the Ottomans and Christians in Europe dragged on for another ten years. In this phase it involved both in a civil war in Transylvania, an area that the Ottomans and their chief rivals, the Christian Hapsburgs, wanted to control. The Hapsburgs supported one side in the civil war and the Turks the other. When the bloody civil war ended in 1606, Transylvania gained some independence. Both the Hapsburgs and Ottomans decided to leave Transylvania alone–for the moment.

THE SPANISH ARMADA

In 1566 an attempt by King Philip II of Spain to tighten his grip on the Spanish-controlled Netherlands led to riots. The rioters were mostly Dutch Protestants and Philip was a Catholic. Philip sent an army of 10,000 men to enforce his reforms, collect taxes, and persecute Dutch Protestants. In 1585 Queen Elizabeth I of England, a Protestant ruler, decided to help the Dutch. The Spanish saw this as a declaration of war and prepared a great fleet—the Armada—to invade England.

The Spanish Armada sails out of port for the English Channel and a series of running battles against the English fleet in 1588.

In 1588 King Philip decided to send a fleet of 130 ships—the Armada—from Spain to the English Channel. The Armada was to link up with the Spanish army in the Netherlands and ferry part of it to England. England was to be conquered.

The naval battle that followed marked the end of one era in naval warfare and the beginning of another. The Spanish ships mounted 2,341 guns, of which 1,100 were heavy weapons. These were used to smash wooden hulls, demast ships, or destroy their cannon. The remainder were chiefly small antipersonnel weapons, used at close range against enemy crews and soldiers.

England's advantages

The Spanish expected to get to close range with the English, grab their warships with grapples, and then fight it out hand-to-hand. The Spanish ships had greater numbers of soldiers on them and would have undoubtedly won this type of battle.

The English, however, were not going to neatly fall in with the Spanish plans. They had a similar number of ships to the Spanish but had the advantage in gunnery. The fleet carried 1,800 cannon, mostly long-range types. The English planned to stay at long range, avoid boarding actions, and pound the Spanish into submission. Many of the English vessels were also

SIR FRANCIS DRAKE

Sir Francis Drake is one of England's greatest national heroes. He made his reputation leading piratical expeditions against Spanish colonies in the Americas. His skills as a seaman were remarkable. He had an instinctive understanding of the sea, its tides, and currents.

Drake was also an imaginative strategist. His raid on Panama in 1572 would have secured a huge hoard of treasure had the Spanish not found his hideout. He also cleverly recognized that Spanish colonies on the west coast of South America were open to attack by a raiding force. In 1577 he sailed there on a voyage that would eventually take him around the world, the first English sailor to accomplish this feat.

One of his greatest naval exploits took place shortly before the Spanish Armada sailed. In an episode described as

To the Spanish he was nothing better than a pirate. To the English Francis Drake was a great patriot and outstanding leader.

"singeing the beard of the king of Spain," Drake sailed into the port of Cadiz in southern Spain at the head of 20 warships. He destroyed 23 Spanish ships.

more maneuverable than their Spanish counterparts and their captains, men like Sir Francis Drake, knew the English Channel's tides and currents extremely well.

The Armada's first sighting of England was made on July 29, 1588. The following day the English fleet, commanded by Admiral Lord Howard, put to sea from Plymouth, southwest England. The Armada moved into its battle formation, a large crescent shape. Fighting between the two fleets began during the mid-morning of the next day.

Long-range gunfire

Howard attacked the rear of the Spanish formation. His ships kept their distance. Their long-range gunfire sank one Spanish ship and damaged several others. The Spanish commander, the Duke of Medina Sidonia, soon realized that the English ships had no intention of slugging it out at close range. He ordered his captains to sail in a defensive circle, believing that this formation would offer a greater degree of protection.

There was no fighting on August 1. The next day, however, the easterly winds favored the Armada. Medina Sidonia turned to attack. Two separate battles, each involving no more than six ships a side, were fought. The two fleets' flagships traded gunfire and more English ships joined the attack on Medina Sidonia's *San Martin*. An officer on the *San Martin* estimated that for 80 shots fired by the Spaniards the English fired 500. The English gunfire had little impact and their ammunition ran low.

With calm winds on August 3 the Spanish fleet was again ready to fight. Admiral Howard knew that the conditions favored the Spaniards so he avoided combat. However, heavy fighting broke out again on the 4th. Howard divided his fleet into four squadrons. The action began early in the morning with an attack by Howard himself on the left of the Armada. Later in the morning the next two squadrons attacked the Spanish center. The battle ended with an attack on the Spanish right by Sir Francis Drake. Once again the English ammunition ran low.

Both sides avoided combat during the next two days. The Armada reached the port of Calais and dropped anchor. Medina Sidonia learned that the army in the Netherlands would not be ready for another week. This was very bad news. The Armada was open to attack while anchored at Calais.

Attacked by fire ships

On the morning of August 7 the English commanders decided to send fire ships against the Spaniards. Fire ships were ordinary vessels packed with materials that burn easily. They were set on fire and sent at enemy ships. Navies in the age of sail frequently used this tactic because wooden ships loaded with gunpowder were very vulnerable to fire. English sailors prepared eight ships from their fleet. As night fell they were sent against the Armada.

Medina Sidonia had expected fire ships. He positioned a number of small boats to tow away any that came near. Only two were successfully turned away, however. To avoid the flames, the Spaniards hurriedly cut their anchors and put to sea. The result of this, in the darkness, was to scatter the Armada.

On the morning of August 8 Medina Sidonia found his flagship under attack by the whole English fleet. Only five other Spanish ships were able to help at first but others joined during

Archers and small cannon on the English warship Ark Royal *pepper a Spanish galleon at close range. Most of the fighting was conducted at longer ranges, where the English fleet's heavier cannon had a decisive advantage.*

the day as the Armada regrouped. The battle lasted nine hours. Not one ship was sunk but many Spanish soldiers and sailors were killed or wounded.

Medina Sidonia wanted to return to Calais but the winds were from the wrong direction. He had to sail north around Britain and Ireland. The Armada met very bad weather. Few Spanish sailors knew the area and dozens of ships were sunk, swamped by mountainous seas or wrecked on rocks. Some 11,000 Spaniards lost their lives, most in the voyage around the British Isles. Over 60 Spanish ships were lost. The English captured or sank 15. Nineteen were lost off the Scottish and Irish coasts. The fate of the remainder is not clear, but most were probably wrecked.

The defeat of the Armada was much celebrated by the English. However, the Spanish continued their war against the Dutch until 1609. The Spanish were also able to put together a new fleet by the summer of 1589. However, the chance of replacing the Protestant monarch in England with a Catholic one vanished with the Armada's defeat, not to be revived for almost a century.

THE THIRTY YEARS WAR

The most terrible war experienced by Europe until the 20th century was caused by an event on May 22, 1618. A group of Protestants in Prague, the capital of the kingdom of Bohemia in Germany, shoved two of the Catholic Holy Roman emperor's close advisers and an official out of a window. The angry Protestants were objecting to a decree signed by the Holy Roman emperor, Matthias, which ended the toleration of the Protestant religion in the empire. The event in Prague sparked a bloody religious war.

Discontented Protestants throw Catholics out of the windows of a royal palace in Prague in 1618. The event sparked the Thirty Years War.

Germany at this time was not a united country, but a collection of 300 states that acknowledged the overlordship of the Catholic Holy Roman emperor. The emperor himself was also king of Bohemia. Some of the states' rulers had adopted the Protestant religion. They had united in 1608 to form the Evangelical Union. In response the Catholic rulers formed the Catholic League in the following year. Protestant and Catholic lived together uneasily until the events of May 1618 in Prague.

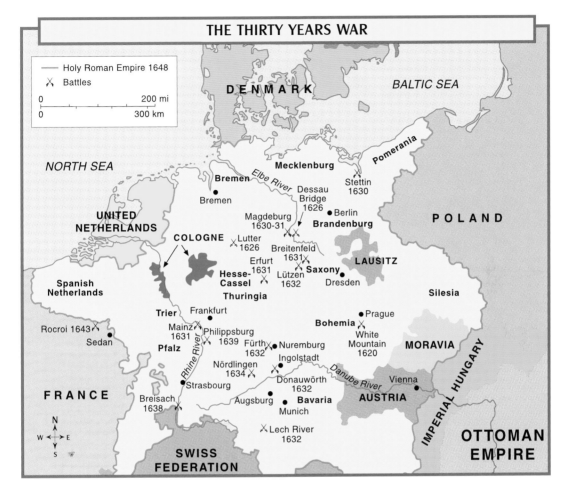

THE THIRTY YEARS WAR

— Holy Roman Empire 1648
✗ Battles

0   200 mi
0   300 km

DENMARK

BALTIC SEA

NORTH SEA

Pomerania

POLAND

Mecklenburg

Bremen
Bremen

Elbe River

Dessau Bridge 1626

Stettin 1630

Magdeburg 1630-31

Berlin
Brandenburg

UNITED NETHERLANDS

COLOGNE

Lutter 1626

Breitenfeld 1631

LAUSITZ

Spanish Netherlands

Erfurt 1631

Hesse-Cassel

Lützen 1632

Saxony
Dresden

Silesia

Thuringia

Trier   Frankfurt

Prague
Bohemia

Rocroi 1643
Sedan

Mainz 1631

Pfalz

Philippsburg 1639

Fürth 1632

Nuremburg

White Mountain 1620

MORAVIA

IMPERIAL HUNGARY

Nördlingen 1634

Ingolstadt

Strasbourg

Donauwörth 1632

Vienna

FRANCE

Breisach 1638

Augsburg

Bavaria
Munich

AUSTRIA

N
W ← → E
S

Lech River 1632

OTTOMAN EMPIRE

SWISS FEDERATION

After Matthias died in March 1619 fighting broke out. The Bohemian Protestants chose a nobleman, Frederick IV, as their king. The Bohemians had already invaded Austria. The Catholic League launched a counterattack. They chose as their general Johan Tserclaes, Count of Tilly. He crushed the main Bohemian army under Prince Christian of Anhalt-Bernberg at the Battle of the White Mountain on November 8, 1620. Prague surrendered.

Frederick's own lands in both western and central Germany were now open to attack. By the summer of 1622 Frederick was living as a refugee at Sedan in France. The combined Bohemian-Evangelical Union army commanded by Count Ernst von Mansfeld, which had once owed loyalty to Frederick, roamed northern Germany and the Netherlands. It supplied itself by stealing from farms and plundering towns in its path.

The Thirty Years War was fought mainly in central Europe and left much of the region in ruins. It was a bitter religious war between Catholics and Protestants, and both sides committed atrocities. Plague and famine added to the misery suffered by ordinary people.

33

GUSTAVUS ADOLPHUS AND HIS ARMY

Gustavus Adolphus, king of Sweden, was an outstanding general and first-rate military innovator. His army was highly professional and easily capable of beating any of its Catholic opponents.

Gustavus Adolphus developed the art of war further than any other European general of the 17th century. In 1612, at the age of 17, he became king of Sweden. Gustavus Adolphus continued a policy of expanding into the territory of Denmark, Poland, and Russia. As a devout Protestant he also was willing to support other Protestants against Catholics.

Gustavus made the Swedish army into an aggressive one on the battlefield. His firearm infantry fired two ranks at a time, instead of the normal one. After the volley, his pike-carrying troops charged, only withdrawing if they failed to achieve a breakthrough. Infantry units also had movable light cannon with them.

The Swedish cavalrymen were trained to charge the enemy, cutting through them with the sword. Gustavus's heavier artillery was easier to move than in rival armies. It could be redeployed on the battlefield to reinforce success or to halt a successful enemy attack.

By the summer of 1623, it looked as if the "Bohemian War" was at an end. The Catholic ruling family of the Holy Roman Empire, the Hapsburgs, had defeated the main Protestant challenge to their policies. But they had received help from Spain, which at the time was at war with France. Cardinal Richelieu, who was the French king's chief minister, made an alliance with several Protestant states, including Denmark and Sweden. In 1625 the war began again.

The Danish king, Christian IV, led an army into Germany. The Holy Roman emperor Ferdinand II had meanwhile hired a mercenary general, Charles Albert von Wallenstein, to command his imperial army. Wallenstein and Tilly cooperated against the two Protestant armies. Mansfeld's army was besieging Dessau when Wallenstein attacked by surprise and defeated him at Dessau Bridge on April 25, 1626. Tilly defeated King Christian IV at the Battle of Lutter on August 27, 1626. The remnants—less than half—of Christian's army fled northward.

Once again the war looked to be at an end. Richelieu made peace with Spain and withdrew from the alliance. Ferdinand II appointed Wallenstein supreme commander of the Baltic Sea. The ambitious mercenary now began attacking the ports on the Baltic. This alarmed the ruler of another Protestant country, one with a small but very good army.

Sweden invades Germany

The king of Sweden, Gustavus Adolphus, received messages from Richelieu warning him that the Holy Roman emperor planned to establish a powerful navy in the Baltic. Gustavus Adolphus decided to invade northern Germany and help his fellow Protestants. On July 10, 1630, he entered the city of Stettin on the Baltic Sea and spent the fall capturing fortresses nearby to secure his long line of supply with Sweden.

In March 1631 Protestant princes in Germany issued a set of demands to the emperor. If they were met, the war would end. These Protestant princes wanted Ferdinand II to stop his campaign against the Protestant faith. Ferdinand rejected their demands. The princes raised a new army and the war resumed.

Catholic troops storm and sack the city of Magdeburg in 1631. The Thirty Years War saw many acts of brutality, but the awful events at Magdeburg stood out. Some 30,000 of the city's citizens were massacred and fire also razed many of its buildings.

Ferdinand dismissed Wallenstein from his service. He was afraid that the wealthy general intended to establish an independent power base. The main Catholic army was now that of Tilly. Since November 1630 it had been besieging Magdeburg. Protestant forces had been using this city as a base. It held large stocks of food that Tilly wanted for his own army. When it fell on May 20, 1631, the besiegers sacked it pitilessly. Thirty thousand people died at the hands of the army or in a fire that started accidentally. The flames also burned the food that Tilly needed.

The sack of Magdeburg stirred up the German Protestants, who now believed they could expect no mercy at the hands of the Catholics. In search of food Tilly withdrew south into Thuringia. He was pursued by Gustavus and his army. The two sides maneuvered for advantage in July and August 1631, before meeting in battle at Breitenfeld on September 17, 1631. Gustavus Adolphus used the superior movability of his army to gain an important victory over Tilly's forces.

Gustavus refused to advance on Vienna. He always believed in having a base from which to get supplies. He spent the winter securing one for next year's campaigns. On September 22 he occupied Erfurt, an important junction of the German system of roads. From here he advanced south and then west. The city of Mainz on the Rhine River surrendered on December 11. He now had a secure base.

A battle for supremacy

The following April Gustavus Adolphus recommenced his march deep into southern Germany, and the emperor called Wallenstein back into service. Two of the greatest commanders of the age, Gustavus and Tilly, would battle for supremacy in the summer of 1632. Gustavus Adolphus planned to invade both Bavaria and Austria from the west, marching along the Danube. His first move was to seize the fortress of Donauwörth on March 27.

Tilly moved his army to the east bank of the Lech River in southern Bavaria, where he built a strong fortified camp. On

Johan Tserclaes, Count of Tilly, was the most able of the Catholic commanders of the Thirty Years War. However, he was responsible for the horrors that followed the capture of Magdeburg. Tilly died from wounds that he received at the Battle of the Lech River in April 1632.

THE BATTLE OF BREITENFELD

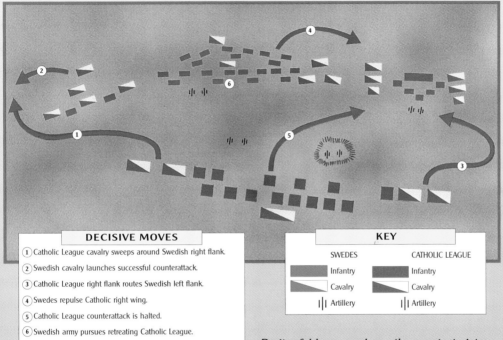

DECISIVE MOVES

1. Catholic League cavalry sweeps around Swedish right flank.
2. Swedish cavalry launches successful counterattack.
3. Catholic League right flank routes Swedish left flank.
4. Swedes repulse Catholic right wing.
5. Catholic League counterattack is halted.
6. Swedish army pursues retreating Catholic League.

KEY

SWEDES		CATHOLIC LEAGUE	
	Infantry		Infantry
	Cavalry		Cavalry
∣∣∣	Artillery	∣∣∣	Artillery

Breitenfeld was perhaps the greatest victory won by Sweden's Gustavus Adolphus over his Catholic enemies.

The army of the Catholic League had captured the Saxon city of Leipzig in 1631. Gustavus Adolphus, however, was advancing toward it with a Swedish and Saxon army. Tilly, the commander of the Catholic League army, deployed his troops for battle at Breitenfeld.

The battle began with an exchange of artillery fire. Next the Catholic cavalry attempted to work around the Swedish right, but were outmaneuvered. Tilly next concentrated his attack on the Saxon forces on the left of Gustavus's army. The Saxons were routed, but Gustavus was able to wheel his army to the right and offset any Catholic advantage.

His army was organized into many small units, with well-trained officers leading them, making it easy to maneuver. This also enabled him to capture the Catholic cannon, which he turned against their former owners. When Gustavus attacked, the Catholic infantry broke and then fled under the weight of the Swedish artillery fire.

Tilly was wounded. His army lost 7,000 killed and 6,000 prisoners out of a total of 36,000. Gustavus had a little over 6,000 men killed and wounded from his army of 42,000 troops.

April 10 Gustavus Adolphus reached the Lech at the city of Augsburg. He had his engineers build a bridge of boats and put his army across the river. On April 16 the Swedes attacked Tilly's camp. Tilly was killed and his army retreated.

The Swedish king had advanced up the Danube to Ingolstadt, a very strong fortress. Gustavus could see no way of taking it that would not end in heavy casualties to his army. He could not

LIGHT ARTILLERY AND MUSKETS

During the 1540s an harquebus with a longer barrel began to appear in the armies of Europe. It was called a musket. It had a longer range and higher bullet speed than the harquebus. Its chief drawback, however, was that it was heavier, requiring a forked rest to support the barrel.

Gustavus Adolphus, however, made a lighter musket and got rid of the forked rest. Better manufacturing techniques meant that the amount of metal in the barrel could be reduced. Gustavus also introduced cartridges. These were paper packets containing a premeasured amount of gunpowder. They made the musket easier to load and more reliable in battle.

Gustavus also made technical improvements to his cannon. Their barrels were also made lighter and cartridges were introduced. He also made an organizational change that was of equal importance. Previously, gunners had been civilian contract workers not subject to military command and control. Gustavus drafted his gunners into the army so that he could train and discipline them like his infantry and cavalry.

Troops, including pikemen and musketeers, dressed in the uniforms that were typical of the Thirty Years War. Individual units were identified by flags and the color of their clothing.

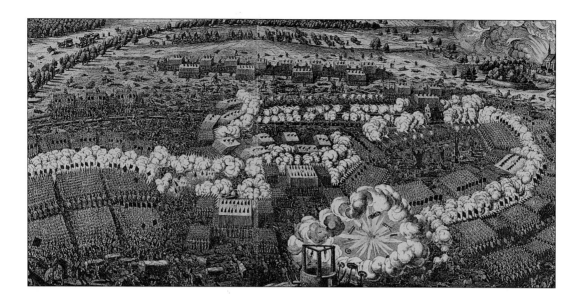

afford to risk such losses so deep in enemy territory. His plan to seize Vienna had to be abandoned. By the end of June he was outside Nuremberg. Tilly's army had retreated northward and was joined by Wallenstein's forces at Fürth on July 11. They constructed a large fortified camp and waited for Gustavus.

Gustavus himself was waiting for reinforcements. His Catholic enemies had around 50,000 soldiers and outnumbered his own forces. He delayed his attack until August, when his strength finally reached 45,000. He launched his first attack on August 31, and on each day thereafter until September 4. Wallenstein had chosen his position well. Gustavus's artillery could not get into a position to bombard the Catholic trenches effectively. His infantry attacks were beaten off with heavy loss.

The death of Gustavus Adolphus

Since he could not fight on his own terms, Gustavus Adolphus broke camp and marched northwestward from Fürth. He had no clear plan of what to do next. Wallenstein took advantage of this unusual indecisiveness and launched an invasion of Saxony, a state allied to Gustavus.

Wallenstein, however, divided his forces. When Gustavus learned of this, he attacked at Lützen. Gustavus led a charge of cavalry supported by infantry against Wallenstein's right. He pushed back the cavalry force here, but Wallenstein attacked in the center and Gustavus turned to reinforce the fighting there.

The Battle of Lützen was fought on November 16, 1632, between Gustavus Adolphus and Wallenstein. The Swedes were victorious, although Gustavus Adolphus was killed. Casualties were heavy on both sides. The Catholics had 12,000 men killed or wounded and the Swedes 10,000.

This German cavalryman is fairly typical of both sides during the Thirty Years War. He wears some armor but his leather jacket was often sufficient protection against sword cuts. Aside from a sword, he has a pair of pistols and might also have carried a type of short musket.

Gustavus was killed in a struggle between infantry and cavalry. The success of the first flank attack, however, put Wallenstein's army in a difficult position. The Swedes forced them to retreat. Both sides suffered heavy casualties, almost half of their armies.

The death of Gustavus Adolphus offered the chance to end the war. In 1633 there were no major military operations, partly because Wallenstein saw he had a chance to take control of all Bohemia. Ferdinand II, however, learned of Wallenstein's secret plans and had his over-mighty commander assassinated on February 23, 1634. On September 6 Wallenstein's army defeated the Swedish forces at the Battle of Nördlingen.

Richelieu, whose policy had been to use other countries to defeat the Hapsburgs in Germany, now decided to enter the war openly. One result was the Peace of Prague, signed in May 1635. Catholic and Protestant rulers in Germany agreed to end the war among themselves and work to drive the Swedes out of Germany.

The capture of fortresses

The main effect of France's joining the war was to change its character. Richelieu entered the war to gain territory for France along the northern and eastern borders of the country at the expense of Spain and the Holy Roman Empire. The campaigns of the following years emphasized the capture of fortresses.

The first gain for France came on December 17, 1638. A French army captured Breisach on the east bank of the Rhine. This river had been a barrier preventing the French from sending their armies into the Holy Roman Empire. However, they were unable to make much use of it immediately. They were also engaged in fighting in the Spanish Netherlands (modern Belgium), northwestern Italy, and in Spain itself. The political and economic strains of warfare now caused revolts in both Spain and France that interfered with their individual war efforts.

In eastern Germany the Swedish army continued its campaign against the Holy Roman emperor. It was brilliantly commanded by Johan Baner, who repeatedly defeated larger armies. However, his army spent each winter taking the food it needed from whatever region of Germany it was using as its base. The war-weary Germans—even the Protestant ones—just wished the Swedish army would go away.

THE PRINCE OF CONDÉ AND THE BATTLE OF ROCROI

The French achieved some success in capturing towns in the Spanish Netherlands between 1638 and 1642. In 1643 a new Spanish commander, Francisco de Melo, decided to attack through the mountainous Ardennes to raid the eastern region of France.

On May 13 he reached the fortress of Rocroi and laid siege to it. The French commander of the armies in this area, Duke Louis d'Enghien, learned of the Spanish advance and chose to attack. At the Battle of Rocroi on May 19 d'Enghien isolated the Spanish infantry by first defeating their cavalry. He then used his artillery to destroy the foot soldiers. Spanish losses were 8,000 dead and 7,000 captured out of 25,000. D'Enghien's casualties were 4,000 from 23,000.

D'Enghien became Prince of Condé in 1646. He was an aggressive commander in the field, but his quarrels with other French nobles provoked a civil war. During the 1650s Condé fought for the Spaniards against the French king. The king and Condé were only reconciled in 1660.

Duke Louis d'Enghien leads the French army to victory at the Battle of Rocroi.

In 1643 the pause in the war caused by unrest in France and Spain ended. A Spanish army from the Netherlands advanced on Paris. It delayed its march to capture the fortress at Rocroi in northeast France. On May 19 a French army defeated the Spanish there. The next year the French captured the Rhine town of Philippsburg. This enabled them to move into Bavaria. However, they found a countryside that could not support an army.

The war in Germany ended after a Swedish invasion of Bavaria in 1648. On October 24, France, the Holy Roman Empire, the German Protestants, and Sweden agreed to peace. France and Sweden gained territory, and the Holy Roman emperor agreed to tolerate Protestants. Bohemia, the cause of the war, had long ago lost its independence to the emperor. Spain and France continued fighting. Their war did not end until 1659.

THE ENGLISH CIVIL WAR

England's Civil War arose from a power struggle between King Charles I and his opponents in Parliament, the center of politics and lawmaking. Charles's attempts to increase his political powers during the 1630s created widespread hostility. His closing of Parliament in 1628, his tax raising methods, lukewarm Protestant beliefs, toleration of Catholicism, and his friendship with the hated Spanish (his wife was a Spanish Catholic) were widely opposed. Charles's break with the Protestants would lead to his downfall.

A light cavalryman (dragoon) from the civil war. Although mounted, he would usually fight on foot, using a cut-down version of the standard musket.

A Scottish rebellion forced Charles to recall Parliament in 1640. Parliament granted him the necessary money to suppress the uprising—but at a price. Charles had to agree to various political and religious reforms in return. However, after Irish Catholics rebelled in 1641 relations between Charles and Parliament became even worse.

Members of Parliament, fearful that Charles had sparked the Irish rebellion in order to raise a force that he would use against them, tried to gain control over the small English army. Puritans, radical Protestants wanting religious and political change, quickly came to influence Parliament. Many moderate politicians, wanting reform not revolution, rallied to the king's camp. The two sides were unable to compromise and England slipped into civil war.

A country divided

Charles's chief support lay mainly in northern and western England, while Parliament's was in the east and south, including the wealthy City of London with its trained bands (militia). Most of England's major ports, such as Bristol, and the navy were in Puritan hands, factors which hindered the amount of foreign support Charles could receive from Catholic countries and wealthy supporters in Europe.

Campaigns were quite fast-moving with armies often marching great distances. Sieges were undertaken but strong fortifications quickly crumbled under artillery fire. There was no dominant weapon on the battlefield. The rate of fire and range of muskets were poor and well-drilled pike formations were often more effective. Cavalry galloping in close order was good for shock action but could not really maneuver in confined areas or make frontal assaults against pikemen. The skill of commanders in selecting favorable ground for a battle and the discipline of their troops often decided engagements. England had no standing army and few professional soldiers at the outset of the war.

The war begins

At the first major battle, Edgehill in October 1642, Parliament tried to stop Charles from reaching London. The engagement was indecisive, although the Parliamentarians had the worst of the fighting. The road to London was left open but Charles failed to seize the opportunity. By the time he advanced, the capital had declared its support for Parliament. The capital's trained bands marched out to confront the king's forces at Turnham Green on November 13. There was a standoff but the king and his supporters, called Royalists, were forced to pull back from London. They had to establish a base in Oxford, which remained their center of operations for the rest of the war.

Royalist successes in battle dominated the campaigns of 1643. The Royalists benefited from aggressive leadership, disciplined cavalry under Prince Rupert, the king's nephew, and the defensive character of Parliamentarian operations due to a general unease felt by many at fighting their sovereign.

The Royalist northern army won a major victory in Yorkshire at Adwalton Moor in June, at Lansdown in the southwest in July, and Rupert took the great port of Bristol the same month. London

Royalist and Puritan cavalry clash at the Battle of Edgehill in 1642. Under Prince Rupert the Royalist cavalry was much more effective than the Puritans' during the first half of the civil war.

now seemed open to Royalist advances from the north, southwest, and Oxford, but Charles wanted to capture the inland port of Gloucester in the west. The city was saved for Parliament by a relief force under the Earl of Essex. On its way back to London Essex's army faced the Royalists at the First Battle of Newbury. The battle was drawn, but Charles fell back to Oxford.

In September a Scottish force, known as Covenanters, joined Parliament. Parliament agreed that the English church would follow the strict Calvinist religious beliefs popular in Scotland in return for this military aid. Charles made an alliance with the Catholic Irish, although it offered little of political or military value. Both Royalists and Parliamentarians were moving further apart and there was little chance of a negotiated settlement to the civil war. Parliament now divided between those wanting a settlement with the king and those wanting complete victory.

The Battle of Marston Moor was fought in northern England on July 2, 1644. Aided by a Scottish army, the Parliamentarians overwhelmed a Royalist army. The victory destroyed the king's support in the north of England.

By the spring of 1644 the Royalists were under great pressure. In May the Earl of Leven led a Scottish force of 21,000 into England to join Sir Thomas Fairfax's northern army and the Earl of Manchester's Eastern Association army in Yorkshire. They besieged the Royalist city of York and Prince Rupert led an army north to relieve it. The Parliamentarians withdrew to cut Rupert off, but he outmaneuvered them and quickly relieved York. However, at Marston Moor in July Rupert's forces, outnumbered by the Parliamentarians, suffered a surprise attack, were routed by well-trained cavalry, and were defeated. This victory gave Parliament control of the north.

The tide slowly turns

In the south Parliament lost the chance to capture Charles in Oxford and end the war. The Parliamentarian armies under the Earl of Essex and Sir William Waller could both have surrounded Oxford. Instead, Essex advanced to the southwest, became isolated, and lost his army at the Battle of Lostwithiel in September. A disagreement developed between the Parliamentarian commanders. The Earl of Manchester became fearful of the revolutionary ideas of his extremist comrades and their threat to social order. He was reluctant to engage his men at the Second Battle of Newbury in October, where Charles, although outnumbered, escaped from the Parliamentarians. Such events showed that a review of Parliamentary forces was needed.

In Scotland the dynamic Marquis of Montrose, leader of the Scottish Royalists, had won the Battle of Tippermuir in September 1644. His victory kept many Covenanters from fighting in England. Montrose then advanced toward the Highlands, occupying several key cities in the mountainous region.

Despite taking the north of England, it was clear that Parliament had to reorganize its armies and leadership to decisively defeat Charles. A major obstacle was the aristocracy in Parliament. They still feared what might happen if the king was

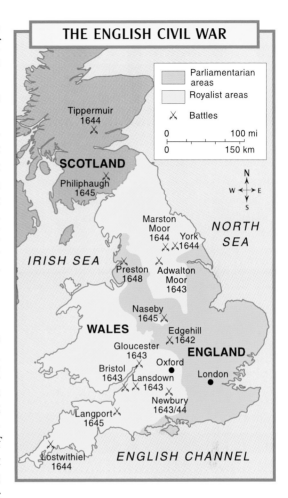

THE ENGLISH CIVIL WAR

Parliamentarian areas
Royalist areas

✕ Battles

0 — 100 mi
0 — 150 km

Tippermuir 1644 ✕

SCOTLAND
Philiphaugh 1645 ✕

Marston Moor 1644 ✕ York ✕ 1644

NORTH SEA

IRISH SEA

Preston 1648 ✕

Adwalton Moor 1643 ✕

Naseby 1645 ✕

WALES

Edgehill ✕ 1642

Gloucester 1643 ✕

ENGLAND

Bristol 1643 ✕

Oxford ●

Lansdown ✕ ✕ 1643

London ●

Newbury 1643/44 ✕

Langport ✕ 1645

Lostwithiel 1644 ✕

ENGLISH CHANNEL

N
W ← → E
S

The civil war divided England between those who supported King Charles and those who championed the rights of Parliament.

THE BATTLE OF NASEBY

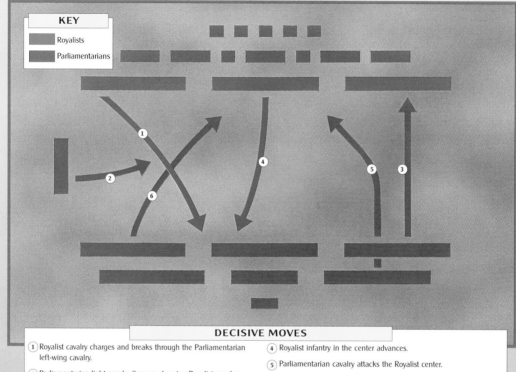

KEY

- Royalists
- Parliamentarians

DECISIVE MOVES

1. Royalist cavalry charges and breaks through the Parliamentarian left-wing cavalry.
2. Parliamentarian light cavalry fires on charging Royalist cavalry.
3. Parliamentarian cavalry smashes Royalist left wing.
4. Royalist infantry in the center advances.
5. Parliamentarian cavalry attacks the Royalist center.
6. Parliamentarian troops advance to complete destruction of the Royalist center.

After Royalist forces in Wales and the southwest failed to move north in the summer of 1645, Prince Rupert was left alone in central England to face the Parliamentarians. Cromwell and Fairfax had an army of 14,000 against the Royalist one of 7,500. Rupert was reluctant to fight but was overruled by other commanders.

The battle opened with a Royalist cavalry charge breaking the left wing of Parliament's line. While the cavalry had disrupted the Parliamentarian wings, the Parliamentarians had men in reserve.

The Battle of Naseby saw the earliest use of the New Model Army, England's first professional standing army.

Soon the greater numbers of the New Model Army began to push back the Royalists. Cromwell's cavalry delivered repeated charges against the Royalist lines, which were severely battered. Despite Charles's efforts to rally his men, the Royalist lines broke. Many of the surviving Royalist troops fled the battlefield but 3,500 were captured.

defeated. Their opponents, however, wanted Charles totally defeated and the country's government completely reorganized. One of the radical Parliamentarians, Oliver Cromwell, gained political support for a "New Model Army," a professional force of infantry, cavalry, and artillery led by professional commanders.

In the spring of 1645 Rupert, now commanding the Royalist forces, tried to resolve the pay and recruitment problems that hampered his armies. Rupert also tried to unify his command but Charles continued to allow his commanders virtual independence.

In 1645 the New Model Army divided. Fairfax, the commander in chief, moved to counter Royalists in the west while Cromwell, commander of its cavalry, harassed Oxford. Rupert marched north, hoping Fairfax would follow and then be isolated. He had planned for Royalists in Wales and the southwest to meet him in the center of England.

The Royalist plan failed. Rupert was left to face a force twice his size as Fairfax and Cromwell moved north together. The armies met at Naseby in June, where Parliament won a decisive victory.

An aerial view of the Battle of Naseby fought on June 14, 1645. The Royalists are at the top of the picture and the Parliamentarians at the bottom. Both sides drew up their forces in the same way, with their infantry in the center and cavalry on the wings.

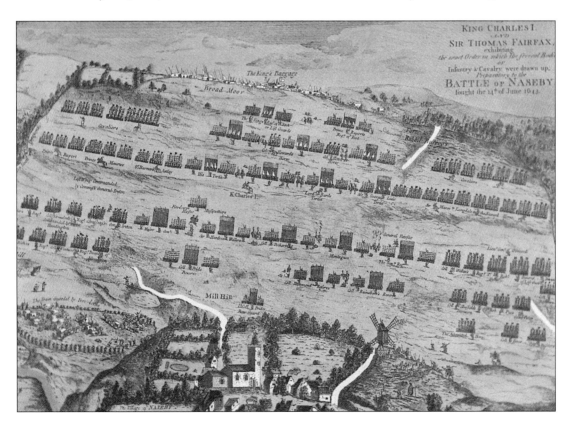

Rupert urged Charles to strengthen his remaining positions in the southwest and negotiate from there. At the same time the New Model Army moved in the same direction and routed Royalists at the Battle of Langport in July.

The Royalists collapse in Scotland

Rupert, besieged in Bristol, surrendered in September. Charles now placed his trust in Montrose in Scotland. By August 1645 Montrose, with an army of never more than a few thousand men and short of artillery and cavalry, had inflicted several major defeats on the Covenanters and resolved to save Charles. Few of his men wanted to go south and his movements were disclosed to Parliament. His forces were crushed at the Battle of Philiphaugh in September. After the collapse of his remaining forces and the loss of Oxford, Charles surrendered to the Scots in July.

Presbyterians in Scotland tried to convert Charles but he resisted and mistakenly believed they would still join him in opposition to the more radical Parliamentarians. Charles was handed over to Parliament, however.

In February 1647 Parliament disbanded the New Model Army, a move that angered troops who had not been paid and wanted to keep their strength together to make sure their demands were met. Cromwell joined the army in mutiny and less radical Parliamentarians were arrested by Cromwell's supporters. Cromwell's negotiations with Charles failed, and when the king escaped to the Isle of Wight, the army radicals demanded revolutionary changes to the English constitution. In December the Scots, fearful of what the changes might mean for Scotland, agreed to fight for Charles and another civil war erupted.

King Charles executed

During the summer of 1648 Royalist uprisings occurred in south Wales and southeast England in expectation of a Scottish invasion. These actions were too soon. In July the Duke of Hamilton led an invading force from Scotland south into England. The poorly led and disunited Royalist uprisings in England were crushed by the New Model Army. Cromwell then moved rapidly north to face a Scottish force twice the size of his army. However, Hamilton's army lacked organization and was short of cavalry, whereas Cromwell's was filled with battle-hardened professionals. The Scots were beaten in a two-day battle around Preston in August. The destruction of Hamilton's army sealed the fate of the king.

Radicals in Parliament then sentenced Charles to death. Charles was executed in January 1649 but Parliament faced serious threats. English politics were still in turmoil, Ireland was in rebellion, and the Scots were angered by the death of the king.

The Parliamentarians had to deal with uprisings in Ireland and Scotland between 1649 and 1652. Both of these were crushed but there were increasing tensions between Parliament and the army. Cromwell assumed virtually dictatorial powers from 1653 until his death five years later. His son Richard took his place briefly but in 1660 Parliament, aided by leading nobles, asked King Charles's son, who later became King Charles II, to accept the throne.

OLIVER CROMWELL AND THE NEW MODEL ARMY

Oliver Cromwell entered Parliament in 1628 and became an outspoken critic of the king. During the civil war he became famous for his leadership of Parliament's Eastern Association army. He raised a well-drilled cavalry force, nicknamed "Ironsides." Cromwell's troopers inflicted a series of defeats upon the Royalists that earned him rapid promotion. In 1645 he was a key figure in selecting new commanders and the creation of the 22,000-strong New Model Army.

It was England's first professional army. Cromwell was chosen to command its cavalry. Cromwell promoted officers who shared his military professionalism and motivation, regardless of their social position. Parliamentarian forces were no longer localized but would operate in any area. More men were recruited and were given uniforms, training, and pay.

The new army became the key to Parliament's victory. It also emerged as a powerful political force. It became the instrument through which Cromwell rose to absolute power and governed England as a virtual dictator.

Oliver Cromwell was the best Parliamentarian general of the civil war and eventually came to rule England as its Lord Protector until his death in 1658.

France's Struggle for Supremacy

Although the Treaty of Westphalia of 1648 ended the Thirty Years War in Germany, France and Spain continued fighting one another. But the high cost of the war started a series of civil wars in France known as the Wars of the Fronde. In January 1650 the chief minister of France, Cardinal Giulio Mazarin, temporarily imprisoned one of his leading opponents, Louis, Prince of Condé. The war resumed in February, when Condé's allies, supported by Spain, raised armies across France to oppose Mazarin.

The Viscount of Turenne was France's greatest general in the expansionist wars of the late 17th century.

At first neither the French royalists nor the rebels waged the war with any skill. In July 1652 the leading royalist general, Henri, Viscount of Turenne, defeated Condé, who had been released from prison in February 1651, outside Paris. Condé retreated to northeastern France. Turenne followed and constructed a fortified camp at Villeneuve-Saint-Georges. Condé refused to attack even though he had a larger army. In October the rebellion collapsed. Condé moved his army to north-central France, where his Spanish allies would find it easier to send help.

End of Spanish supremacy

In 1654 Condé convinced his Spanish allies to lay siege to the town of Arras in northeast France. A Spanish army arrived in July. However, the Spaniards spent more time digging their siege works than trying to attack the town. This allowed Turenne to march to the aid of Arras. On August 25 Turenne led a night attack on the Spanish and routed them. Condé avenged the defeat at Arras by destroying a royalist army besieging Valenciennes in northeast France on July 16, 1656.

In 1655 an English expedition to the West Indies had captured Jamaica. Spain declared war on its old enemy. France and England allied against their common

THE BATTLE OF THE DUNES

Henri de la Tour d'Auvergne, Viscount of Turenne, was a skillful commander. An example of his ability to adapt his army to the terrain is provided by the Battle of the Dunes. A Spanish army of 16,000 men attempting to break the siege of Dunkirk drew up for battle on June 14, 1658. Its right flank rested on a beach.

Turenne, at the head of 15,000 men, realized that as the tide went out he would gain more space for his cavalry to sweep around the Spanish flank. This enabled him to surround the enemy army and achieve a crushing victory.

The battle last four hours. Some 6,000 Spaniards were killed or captured, for a loss of only 400 French and English. Dunkirk, with no hope of relief, surrendered to Turenne. His death in July 1675 was a major loss to the French army.

Turenne leads the final advance of the Anglo-French forces against the defeated Spanish at the Battle of the Dunes.

opponent in 1657. A small English force arrived in France and the combined Anglo-French army laid siege to the Spanish-held port of Dunkirk. The Spaniards marched to relieve the siege but were defeated at the Battle of the Dunes in June 1658.

The victory at the Dunes allowed the French to take most of the fortresses along their border with the Spanish Netherlands. With the war obviously lost the Spaniards asked for peace terms. The Peace of the Pyrenees, signed between France and Spain in November 1659, ended the war between the two that had lasted for 25 years. Spain's supremacy in Europe, which had begun 150 years earlier, had ended.

Expanding France's frontiers

King Louis XIV of France now tried to replace Spain as the major power in Europe. He began a series of wars that had two overall objectives: to control the Spanish Netherlands and to advance

France's eastern border to the Rhine River. Because the wars were fought to expand the territory of France, they continued to focus on the capture of frontier fortresses and towns.

The first was a very short war against Spain, the War of Devolution between 1667 and 1668. Turenne invaded the Spanish Netherlands and captured a number of fortresses. Meanwhile Condé, who had been allowed to return to French service, captured the Spanish-controlled region known as Franche-Comté. The war ended with Turenne's conquests being held, but Franche-Comté was returned to Spain.

Dutch calls for help

The independent Netherlands had no desire to see France control the Spanish Netherlands. Louis XIV organized an alliance against them, which included England and some small German states. In March 1672 he declared war. When the French army invaded the Netherlands in May, the Dutch opened the dikes that kept the North Sea from flooding their county. It was a desperate measure, but it halted the French army.

The Dutch convinced Leopold I, the Holy Roman emperor, Charles II of Spain; and the ruler of the German state of Brandenburg to join them against Louis. This gave Louis an excuse to attack in the Spanish Netherlands and along the Rhine River. Turenne's campaign in the Rhineland from 1674 to 1675 saw him outmaneuver his enemies. Their defensive tactics in battle, in spite of their greater numbers, allowed Turenne to triumph time and again. However, Turenne was killed by a stray cannonball at the Battle of Sassbach near Strasbourg on July 27, 1675, while preparing his forces for an attack.

The war continued for three more years, until Louis's financial minister convinced him that the cost would destroy France. The peace treaties ending it were signed between 1678 and 1679. France had gained territory in both the north and east.

The rest of Europe now combined against Louis, fearing that he was determined to conquer even more of Europe. An anti-French alliance, the League of Augsburg, was agreed on in July 1686. Louis could have avoided war but he chose to invade Germany in September 1688 instead. His one ally, Catholic James II of England, lost his throne in December 1688, when a Protestant, later King William III, was invited to take the English crown by those who were opposed to James's attempts to impose Catholicism on England. James II crossed to Ireland in 1689.

War between France and Spain, England, the Netherlands, and the Holy Roman Empire began in 1689. In 1690 Louis's forces gained victories over the Anglo-Dutch fleet at the Battle of Beachy Head off the south coast of England and the allied army in Italy. But the defeat of James II, the former king of England, and his army of Catholic followers at the Battle of the Boyne in Ireland in July lost Louis his chance of victory against England.

Defeat at sea, success on land

The course of the war very gradually came to favor the allies. In 1692 an Anglo-Dutch naval victory at La Hougue off the northern coast of France saw the French lose 15 warships. These losses became decisive because the French could not afford to replace their warships. Louis had to abandon his plans to invade England because of the defeat at La Hougue. The French armies in the Spanish Netherlands, northwestern Italy, and northeastern Spain needed most of the government's money to pay for their campaigns. There was no money available in the French treasury for new warships, no matter how much they were needed.

King William III of England leads his Protestant Anglo-Dutch forces to victory over the deposed Catholic King James II of England at the Battle of the Boyne in 1690. William's victory ended any chance of a revival of Catholic fortunes in England.

THE BATTLE OF THE BOYNE

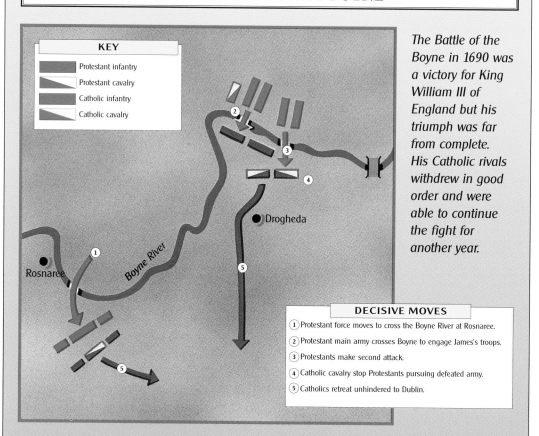

KEY

- Protestant infantry
- Protestant cavalry
- Catholic infantry
- Catholic cavalry

Drogheda

Boyne River

Rosnaree

The Battle of the Boyne in 1690 was a victory for King William III of England but his triumph was far from complete. His Catholic rivals withdrew in good order and were able to continue the fight for another year.

DECISIVE MOVES

1. Protestant force moves to cross the Boyne River at Rosnaree.
2. Protestant main army crosses Boyne to engage James's troops.
3. Protestants make second attack.
4. Catholic cavalry stop Protestants pursuing defeated army.
5. Catholics retreat unhindered to Dublin.

The Battle of the Boyne in 1690 sealed Ireland's fate to be a nation divided by religion. Deposed Catholic King James II attempted to recover part of his former kingdoms of Ireland, Scotland, and England. He commanded a poor-quality Franco-Irish army of 23,000 opposed by a Anglo-Dutch and Scots-Irish army of 34,000 led by Protestant King William III. The Boyne River separated the two armies. The Catholics were in a strong position. They occupied a low hill and dug earthwork fortifications.

William sent a quarter of his force to find a ford about six miles (9.6 km) from the Franco-Irish left. James saw the troop movement and sent a similar-sized force to block it. William's army then pushed across the river, and drove the Irish infantry out of their defenses.

A follow-up attack on the right flank of the Irish fall-back position succeeded and James's infantry retreated. The Irish cavalry kept William's army from pursuing too closely. James fled back to France after the defeat.

In fact on land France was doing very well. Arguments between allied commanders in Italy prevented them from accomplishing anything. In the Netherlands the French army won victories at Steenkerke in 1692 and Neerwinden the following year. At Steenkerke the French fought behind trenches and earthworks and the allies failed to break through them before being forced to retreat by French counterattacks.

At Neerwinden it was the allies who fought from behind trenches and earthworks but they were finally beaten after a French cavalry charge penetrated their defenses. The French casualties amounted to some 9,000 men, while the allies lost significantly more, 19,000.

The naval Battle of La Hougue was fought between French and Anglo-Dutch fleets in 1692. It ended with a resounding defeat for the French. They had over a dozen warships sunk and had to abandon their plans to invade England with an army of 30,000 men.

An end to the fighting

In Spain, Barcelona was besieged by the French in 1694 but the arrival of an English fleet postponed its surrender until 1697. By this time the cost of the war weighed heavily on all the contestants and most were looking to end the conflict. In the fall of 1697 the Treaty of Ryswick took away all France's gains except for the city of Strasbourg.

FORTS AND SIEGE WARFARE

The 17th century was an era in which armies grew larger than ever before. The quantity of food and other supplies they needed could not be provided from the countryside through which they marched. Chains of fortified towns and "magazines"—fortified supply bases—were built to guard the main roads the armies traveled along and to protect a country's frontiers. The capture of these fortresses would destroy an enemy's lines of communication. Sieges and fortifications therefore became key factors in warfare.

Vauban was the greatest military engineer of his age and added a new dimension to both warfare and military engineering.

As a result of all these factors the construction and taking of fortresses came to be two of the main objectives in warfare. Marshal Sébastien le Prestre de Vauban dominated fortification and siege warfare during the reign of King Louis XIV of France. Vauban took ideas about fortresses that emerged in the mid-16th century, combined them with his skill in geometry and a practical eye for the area involved, to produce new siege techniques.

His fortifications used a design that surrounded the main body of a fortress with a series of ditches, low walls, and earthworks. The key innovation was the use of earth. Stone walls shattered under the impact of artillery fire. Earth, being less rigid, absorbed the force.

Fire from three directions

Vauban also added small triangular forts beyond the walls of a fortress that were arranged in such a way as to ensure that any attack on a main wall faced fire from three directions. Attackers had to break through a defensive system covered with obstacles. Vauban improved the forts along the French frontiers.

Siege warfare also advanced under the French engineer, who personally directed some 50 operations. Artillery in earlier sieges fired at long ranges, while sappers (skilled tunnelers) approached the walls along zigzag trenches (saps). The zigzag

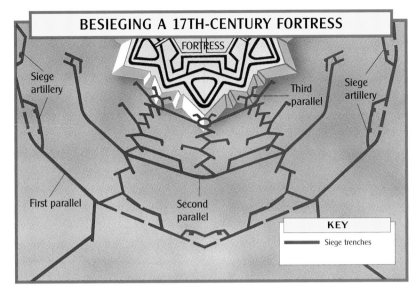

BESIEGING A 17TH-CENTURY FORTRESS

FORTRESS

Siege artillery

Third parallel

Siege artillery

First parallel

Second parallel

KEY

Siege trenches

A typical system of siege lines around a Vauban-style fortress. Covered by artillery batteries sited in parallel trenches, zigzag saps are dug ever closer to the walls of the fortress.

prevented the defenders from firing directly down the length of the trench. Vauban protected his siege lines by first making sure that cavalry cleared surrounding districts and blocked all access roads. He then introduced a system of trenches running parallel to the fortress walls.

Parallel trench lines

Long-range artillery covered the digging of saps and a second parallel trench line. More artillery and mortars then came forward to give covering fire for a third parallel trench before a final bombardment to breach the walls began. These parallel lines enabled more fire to be directed against the defenders, gave greater protection to the sappers, and increased the opportunity for simultaneous attacks from different points.

Although military engineering required skill and became crucial in warfare, aristocrats considered it beneath their dignity. Vauban was denied the promotions enjoyed by aristocratic officers. Vauban finally had to make a request in writing before he was promoted to the rank of marshal in 1703.

Vauban's technical writing made his system of fortifications a key element in military studies across Europe for over a century. His book *On Siege and Fortification* was printed in 1737 and again in 1829. His methods were still being used in the middle of the 19th century. As artillery increased in range, accuracy, and quantity, Vauban's fortress system became obsolete, however.

THE ANGLO-DUTCH NAVAL WARS

Commercial rivalry between England and the Netherlands turned into a series of naval conflicts in the second half of the 17th century. In May 1652 an English fleet commanded by Robert Blake tried to search a Dutch convoy. A large Dutch squadron of warships commanded by Marten Tromp stopped him. The two fleets exchanged gunfire for several hours. The Dutch withdrew after losing two ships. War was declared in July. It was the first of several naval wars fought between England and the Netherlands.

English and Dutch warships clash off the coast of England on February 18, 1653.

In September Blake engaged another Dutch fleet off the north coast of Kent, England. He defeated the Dutch so heavily that the English believed campaigning for the year was over. However, Tromp defeated Blake's heavily outnumbered fleet off Dungeness, Sussex, in November 1652.

In February 1653 the passage of a Dutch convoy through the English Channel provoked a fight. Blake beat Tromp. Worse was to follow. Superior English tactics won the Battle of Scheveningen off the Dutch coast on July 31 and Tromp was killed. The Dutch agreed to peace.

Economic rivalries also led to the Second Anglo-Dutch War. A Dutch attack on a convoy of English merchant ships on June 3, 1665, led to the Battle of Lowestoft. The Dutch were driven off after losing over 30 ships.

The next year the Dutch gained France as an ally. The English fleet divided to deal with the threat. Part sailed west to protect against a French attack. This meant the Dutch fleet outnumbered the English eastern squadron. The Dutch attacked on June 11, 1666. The Four Days Battle saw the English suffer 20 ships sunk.

In 1667 the English government was so short of money that it disbanded the

ENGLAND'S FIGHTING INSTRUCTIONS

In the smoke and confusion of a naval action an admiral more or less surrendered control over his fleet. The only way to communicate was by shouting or by signaling using lanterns or flags. It was impossible for a ship at the front of a line of warships to expect an order to be easily understood by the last ship.

The English navy tackled the problem in March 1653. Parliament approved a set of rules known as *Fighting Instructions.*

These took the form of a small book that all ships carried. Numbered short paragraphs instructed captains what to do in certain situations.

Under Instruction 21, for example: "None of the ships of the fleet shall pursue any small number of the enemy's ships, till the main body be disabled or run." Some also included descriptions of flag or gunfire signals that the admiral's ship might make.

fleet. The Dutch admiral, Michel de Ruyter, saw his chance. He entered the Medway—the mouth of the Thames River—got close to London, and burned the dockyard at Chatham. The war ended on terms favorable to the Dutch.

An unpopular war

The Third Anglo-Dutch War was part of France's war against its former Dutch ally. The French allied with the English. Their fleets were attacked by de Ruyter at Sole Bay off the east coast of England on May 28, 1672. The French withdrew and the English suffered heavily before help arrived. In 1673 de Ruyter won victories, at Schooneveldt Channel, the mouth of a river in the southwest Netherlands, and Texel, a Dutch island in the North Sea. The war was unpopular in England, however, and a peace was negotiated that finally ended the long conflict.

A scene from the Four Days Battle in June 1666. An English warship (draped in white flags) surrenders to the victorious Dutch.

SWEDEN'S WARS OF EXPANSION

In 1655 Sweden possessed a Baltic empire that included most of what is now Finland, Estonia, Livonia, and the area of what is now modern Russia around St. Petersburg. In 1654 the Swedish government discovered that the country's monarch, Queen Christina, had been secretly converted from the country's official Protestant faith to the Catholic one. Since it was illegal to be a Catholic in Sweden, she was sent into exile. Charles X became king in her place. Charles was an aggressive ruler and decided to expand his country.

Charles saw that Poland was politically weak. It was also losing a war with Russia. Charles believed he could add Poland to Sweden's territory. Charles informed the Polish king, John Casimir, that he, Charles, was Protector of Poland. John Casimir refused to accept Charles's offer of military help. Charles, believing that Poland would be easily conquered, declared war in 1655.

The Poles were too disorganized to defend against Charles's attack. On August 29 the Swedes entered Warsaw, the capital, and then pressed on southward. The Poles defended Cracow for two weeks before evacuating the city. John Casimir fled and the Swedes now occupied the country. The Poles were expected to feed the Swedish army. If the Swedes did not get enough food from a town, they would plunder it.

The Dutch fleet engages the Swedish ships blockading Copenhagen, the Danish capital, on November 1, 1658. The Dutch were able to break through and temporarily relieved Copenhagen.

Russia's Army

The wars of Czar Aleksei Mikhailovich Romanov against Poland and Sweden were a sign of Russia's intention to expand into Eastern Europe in the 17th century. However, much of the czar's army was of poor quality.

Russia's best troops were supposed to be the streltsi (musketeers). They had been founded in 1550. The streltsi were armed with large axes and muskets. However, by Aleksei's time the streltsi had lost their fighting efficiency.

Aleksei increasingly relied on masses of peasants, who were herded from their villages, put into uniform, and sent straight to the battlefield. Their officers also had little military experience.

Three Russian streltsi armed with their traditional weapons of musket and long-handled ax.

In 1656 Poland rose in a general rebellion against the Swedes. Armed bands made attacks against Swedish garrisons. John Casimir returned from exile and assembled an army to recapture Warsaw. The Poles attacked with such fury that the Swedes surrendered even though they had defeated two assaults.

The war widens

The war in Poland now drew in countries bordering Poland's frontiers. Prussians, Transylvanians, and Russians all invaded Poland or Swedish territories on the shores of the Baltic Sea between 1656 and 1657. The Russians attacked Riga, a Baltic seaport, but were defeated in August 1658. When Denmark joined the war as an ally of Poland, Charles attacked Denmark.

Charles caught the Danes completely unprepared. He conquered the region of Jutland in mid-1657. But his attempted assault on Copenhagen in July 1658 was driven off by the Danes. The Dutch sent a fleet to help the Danes in November 1658, and Charles's hopes of victory faded. After Charles died of fever in 1660, the Swedish government made peace with all its neighbors.

THE OTTOMANS IN DECLINE

During the 17th century the Ottoman Empire waged largely defensive wars to protect its territories in Europe. The expansion of the empire had been halted by the Christian European states at Malta in 1565 and Lepanto in 1571 (see pages 23–27). The state of the empire is best shown by the 1606 treaty ending a long war. Under its terms the money the Holy Roman emperor paid to the Turks was stopped. The sultan was forced to accept his Hapsburg neighbor in the Balkans as an equal. The Ottoman Empire was slowly declining.

Two types of soldier serving with the Ottomans. From left to right: an artilleryman and a Janissary. The Ottomans could raise large armies but only the elite Janissaries, their artillery, and some cavalry were trained soldiers.

The Ottoman sultans had brought the northern coast of the Black Sea under their rule during the 15th century. The sea's northern coast bordered on the Polish-controlled Ukraine, where Cossack bands (Russian cavalrymen) roamed. Raids by one Cossack band into Ottoman territory caused a Turkish invasion that led to a Polish-Turkish war between 1620 and 1621. Neither side gained an advantage from the conflict. In 1621 Poland and the Turkish sultan, Osman II, agreed to a truce that halted the war, although the Cossack raids into Turkish territory continued.

The Janissaries revolt

Osman returned to the Turkish capital, Constantinople. Turkey faced increasing difficulties controlling its subject peoples and defending its borders. Osman attempted to tighten up his control over the country by removing some of the privileges held by the Janissaries, the elite corps of Turkish infantry. The Janissaries objected and overthrew Osman, replacing him with his more easily controlled brother. The Janissaries effectively dominated the Turkish government for the next 30 years.

In 1645 ships sailing from the Venetian-controlled island of Crete captured a Turkish vessel carrying the wives of the Turkish sultan, Ibrahim I. Christian sea captains such as the Venetians had for long preyed on Turkish shipping. The Turks decided to end this menace once and for all. A huge army estimated at between 50,000 and 75,000 men was transported to Crete. The Turks, aided by the local Greeks who hated the Venetians, captured two of the three major fortresses in Crete: Canea fell in 1645 and Retino in 1646. When they began the siege of Candia in 1648, the Turks had little idea how long the city would take to capture.

The Turkish navy defeated

A considerable part of the wealth of the Venetian Republic came from a spice market on the island of Chios in the Aegean Sea. Crete provided vital ports for galleys on the journey between Chios and Venice. The Venetians did all they could to keep Candia supplied during the Turkish siege.

The Venetian navy was much better than the Turkish. This Venetian naval supremacy kept Candia's garrison supplied with food and ammunition. The Turkish army's own supply lines were cut by the Venetian fleet. In 1649 the Venetians sailed up to the Dardanelles, the straits between Asia Minor and Europe, and defeated the Turkish navy. The Venetians blockaded the straits so that Turkish ships could not sail between Constantinople and the Mediterranean ports. The stalemate continued until 1656, when the Turks made another attempt to break the blockade. Again they were defeated by the Venetian fleet, which could have sailed up to Constantinople itself had not a lucky shot from a shore battery destroyed its flagship.

The battle for Transylvania

In 1656, a new grand vizier, or chief minister, took control of the Turkish government. Mohammed Koprulu tried to reverse the slow decline of the empire. He reorganized the Turkish fleet, which in 1657 was able at last to defeat the Venetians and break the blockade. The Turks then sailed into the Mediterranean and captured several Venetian-held islands in the Aegean Sea.

Koprulu also intervened in Transylvania. The ruler of this semi-independent part of the Ottoman Empire (now part of Romania), George Rakoczy, with the support of the Holy Roman emperor, ignored Turkish rule over his realm. The Turks sent an army to remove Rakoczy but he defeated it at the Battle of Lippa in Transylvania in May 1658. After Crimean Tartars (descendants of the Asiatic Mongols) arrived to reinforce the Turks, Rakoczy fled to Hapsburg Hungary. He returned the next year and drove out his Turkish-backed replacement, only to suffer defeat in 1660 at the Battle of Fenes in Transylvania. Rakoczy was killed. His successor, Janos Kemeny, was killed at the Battle of Nagyszollos also in Transylvania in January 1662.

The Turks took direct control of Transylvania and then invaded the Holy Roman Empire. At the Battle of the Raab River in Hungary in August 1664 an imperial army halted the Turks. Koprulu had died but his son, Fazil Ahmed Koprulu, continued his policies. The treaty that ended this war in 1664 made sure that Transylvania remained part of the Ottoman Empire.

The empire under threat

Candia was still under siege as these events unfolded. Under Fazil Ahmed Koprulu, the Cretan fortress finally surrendered in 1669. By the terms of the treaty ending the war, Venice lost Crete and its Aegean islands. But there was no rest for the Ottoman Turks.

A war against Poland between 1671 and 1677 added territory in the Ukraine to the empire. This was lost at the end of a war with Russia in 1681. The Polish war had led to the election of the great general Jan Sobieski as the king of Poland. He believed that

JAN SOBIESKI

Jan Sobieski was a Polish nobleman. He had achieved military success fighting the Tartars in the Ukraine, when he took command of a large Polish army to counter the Turkish invasion of the western Ukraine in 1673.

Over the next three years he won three major victories over the Turks. The first, at Chocin in Poland on November 11, 1673, saw his army annihilate a Turkish force of 40,000. His victory won him friends in high places. He was made the king of Poland. His next two victories in Poland, at Lwow in 1675 and Zorawno in 1676, were won against larger Turkish armies.

Sobieski's greatest strength was his strategic vision. The alliance he made with the Holy Roman Empire against the Turks in March 1683, together with his march to help defend Vienna from Turkish attack that summer, gave the city's defenders the edge they needed to beat the Turks.

Polish nobleman Jan Sobieski was a skilled general and able diplomat. He won several victories over the Turks and was rewarded with the Polish crown.

Turkey would sooner or later attack Poland again. He signed an alliance with the Holy Roman Empire in March 1683 knowing that the alliance offered the best chance of defeating the Turks.

However, popular unrest in Hungary alarmed Sobieski. The part of Hungary ruled by the Hapsburgs had rebelled against its rulers in 1678. Concessions made by the emperor removed a lot of the rebels' popular support and they turned to the Turks for help. In 1682 Kara Mustafa Koprulu demanded that the Holy Roman Empire grant independence to Hungary. When the

THE SIEGE OF VIENNA

The Turkish Grand Vizier Kara Mustafa invaded the Holy Roman Empire in June 1683 with an army of 200,000 soldiers. He arrived outside Vienna on July 14. Lacking heavy artillery, Count Rudiger von Starhemberg defended Vienna with a garrison of 15,000. He kept the Turkish besiegers off balance with frequent attacks on their defenses.

In late August Jan Sobieski left Warsaw with 30,000 soldiers and marched quickly toward Vienna. He and his army covered 220 miles (352 km) in 15 days. The Polish army met with allied German and Austrian forces near Vienna. The combined allied army of 75,000 attacked the Turks on September 12.

The infantry attacked the Turkish defenses late in the afternoon and the Vienna garrison joined in. The fighting was indecisive. Sobieski then led a sudden cavalry charge on the enemy command post that caused the whole Turkish army to retreat in confusion.

Vienna at the time of the Turkish siege in 1683. The city held out and the Turks suffered heavy losses before retreating.

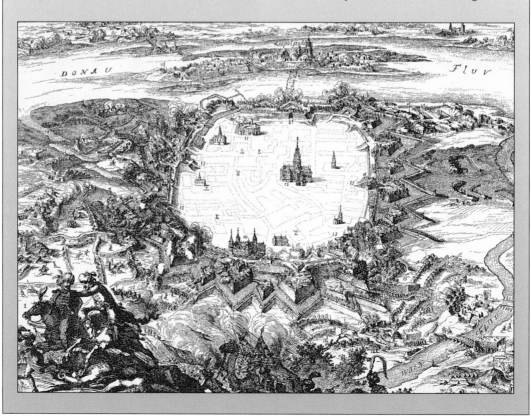

emperor refused, a huge Turkish invasion force laid siege to Vienna in 1683. Sobieski's help was vital in defeating the Turks. They lost heavily but escaped complete destruction because they were not pursued by Sobieski who feared being ambushed.

Turkish ambitions thwarted

The Battle of Vienna marked the end of the Turkish threat to central Europe. The last years of the 17th century saw the Holy League, made up of the Holy Roman Empire, Venice, and Poland make many territorial gains at Turkish expense. Although the Turks recovered some territory, their defeat at the Battle of Zenta in Hungary in 1697 handed Hungary and Transylvania to the Holy Roman emperor. The Turks invaded Hungary from Belgrade led by Sultan Mustafa II but were virtually annihilated at Zenta by a European force led by Prince Eugene of Savoy, a state in northern Italy. After the Battle of Zenta the Turks never again attempted an invasion of central Europe.

The Ottoman Empire continued until the 20th century but the era of its greatness ended at the close of the 17th. Never again would the Turks break out from the Balkans. The Balkan countries, however, would try to overthrow their Turkish masters.

The Turkish army besieging Vienna in 1683 is attacked by a relief force led by Jan Sobieski. Sobieski attacked late in the afternoon of September 12. Aided by the city's defenders, Sobieski crushed the Turkish besiegers.

THE MANCHU EMPIRE

Northeast of the Great Wall of China, in the land of Manchuria, lived a nomadic people known as the Juchen. They first appear in recorded Chinese history during the 12th century. They were part of the Mongol Empire. When the Ming dynasty regained control of China, the Juchen won a measure of independence. The Chinese organized them into tribal groups with hereditary leaders. The Juchen, however, were destined to overthrow the Ming and establish the great Manchu Empire.

Emperor K'ang-hsi was responsible for the creation of a stable Manchu regime in China during the late 1600s.

During the 16th century the Juchen gradually became like the Chinese. They began to farm the land and live in towns and cities. In 1582 a civil war broke out in one of the Juchen tribal groups, the Chien-chou. In 1583 a young man named Nurhachi became the Chien-chou's leader. Nurhachi was ambitious for himself and his people. He united all the Juchen under his leadership. He carefully maintained his loyalty to the Chinese emperor until he was ready to challenge for the throne. He fortified his capital and created a standing army.

In 1616 Nurhachi proclaimed himself the "Heaven's-designated emperor." He issued a long list of complaints against the Chinese and began a war against the Ming by seizing the city of Fushun. The Ming emperor, Shen Tsung, sent an army of 90,000 soldiers commanded by Yang Hao to punish Nurhachi. Nurhachi defeated it easily. He captured the towns of Liaoyang and Mukden in 1621. He moved his capital to Mukden in 1625.

Nurhachi defeated

In 1626 a Ming provincial governor, Yuang Ch'unghuan, was able to defeat Nurhachi thanks to his artillery, which had been organized with the help of European Christian missionaries. Nurhachi died about seven months later of disease and, it was said, of a broken heart. He left capable successors, however. These took the name Manchu in 1636.

The Ming, with the help of European mercenaries and missionaries, could have defeated the Manchu easily. However, some Chinese disliked the westerners and they did all they could to keep them from helping. In 1637, for example, a Ming official hired 400 Portuguese gunners but other government officials refused to do the legal paperwork needed to get them to the battlefront.

Further Manchu expansion

Two peasant rebellions in northern and central China broke out at the same time in 1626. They each produced a wandering band of rebel soldiers that interfered with the collection of taxes. In 1644 one of these peasant bands captured Beijing because the Ming leaders had left their capital unprotected. The last Ming emperor killed himself.

A Chinese general now joined forces with the Manchu to defeat the peasants. At a major battle close to the Great Wall, the Manchu army defeated the peasant rebels. When the combined army occupied Beijing, the Manchu leader, Dorgon, made his capital there and the Manchu became masters of northern China.

THE MANCHU ARMY

Nurhachi reorganized the Juchen army in 1601. He created four companies (banners), each of 300 soldiers. Each was named for the colored flag it carried into battle. These were yellow, white, blue, and red. As more and more of the Juchen acknowledged Nurhachi's rule, they became part of a banner. Army officers were drawn from the Manchu nobility, rather than tribal chieftains. By 1615 there were 200 companies in the Manchu army. Four more banners were added to the original four to make the army's organization more flexible.

The Manchu army, both infantry and cavalry, was mainly equipped with bows, spears, swords, and shields at first, but the army benefited from contact with Europeans, particularly traders and those with military experience. The Europeans provided muskets and cannon and taught the Manchu troops how to use them in battle. The Manchu army became one of the best fighting forces in Asia.

Between 1645 and 1683 the Manchu gradually gained control of all China. Under the Manchus, particularly K'ang-hsi who ruled from 1662 to 1722, China gained a measure of stability previously unknown and continued to expand. The last place to fall was the island of Taiwan in 1683, where some Ming loyalists had founded a pirate kingdom. The Manchus also tried to expand their frontiers into other neighboring territories. The independent Mongols were conquered in 1696, partly due to K'ang-hsi's victory at Urga in Mongolia. Genghis Khan's onetime subjects now ruled over the great Mongol leader's descendants.

THE WARS OF
SAFAVID PERSIA

Ismail I, the founder of the Safavid dynasty in Persia (modern Iran), began by defeating the Ottomans who ruled in western Persia. By 1510 Ismail I controlled all of Persia and a part of Afghanistan to the east. The growth of Persian power alarmed Selim, the Ottoman Turkish ruler. The Turks also saw the Persians as heretical Muslims, since they followed the type of Islam known as Shiah. The Turks were of the Muslim Sunni faith. This friction was a recipe for a bitter and long religious war.

A Safavid Persian general from the 17th century. Until the arrival of European gunpowder weapons, such mounted warriors dominated Persian armies.

The conflict between Persia and Turkey intensified in 1526. The Persians first recovered most of the land the Turks had conquered under Selim (see pages 20–21). The response of the new Ottoman emperor, Suleiman the Magnificent, was to invade Persia again in 1533. He first struck north into Azerbaijan. When he turned south to Mesopotamia, the Persians regained Azerbaijan. The Turks were unable to hang on to their conquests because the fighting was at the end of their supply lines. Too little food and weapons were reaching them. In 1555 the war was brought to an end.

Turkish successes

The Turks resumed the war in 1577. This time whenever they captured an important city they fortified it. They were now able to keep stockpiles of supplies close to Persia, making their armies more successful. At the end of the war they controlled most of western Persia.

In 1587 Shah Abbas I gained the Persian throne. He went to war with Turkey in 1602. He recovered all Persia's lost lands by 1604. The Turkish counter-attacking army was destroyed at the Battle of Sis in 1606. Abbas sent a strong force around the rear of the Turks. The Turks thought this was the main attack and turned to face it. Abbas now launched his main attack against the Turks from what had been their front. It was a route. Some 20,000 Turks—about one-fifth of the total— were killed in the battle. A treaty recognizing Persia's victory was signed in 1612. The Turks twice tried to avenge their defeats at the hands of Abbas. In the second war, fought between 1623 and 1638, they captured Baghdad and kept it under the terms of the treaty that ended the war.

After Abbas, Safavid Persia declined slowly under a succession of weak rulers. A revolt in the Afghan provinces led to a civil war in the 1720s. The last two shahs were both figurehead rulers. Real power was in the hands of Nadir Kuli Beg. He repeatedly defeated the Turks. In 1736 he was elected shah himself. In 1738 Nadir successfully invaded India, after the ruler there had aided an Afghan revolt.

Nadir was a Sunni Muslim. He tried to make Shiah Persia abandon the religion he considered a false one. As a result he was assassinated by his own men. Persia entered a period of destructive civil war. The Safavid Empire was no more.

The Safavid Persian Empire flourished from the early 16th century until it collapsed due to religious infighting during the middle of the 18th century.

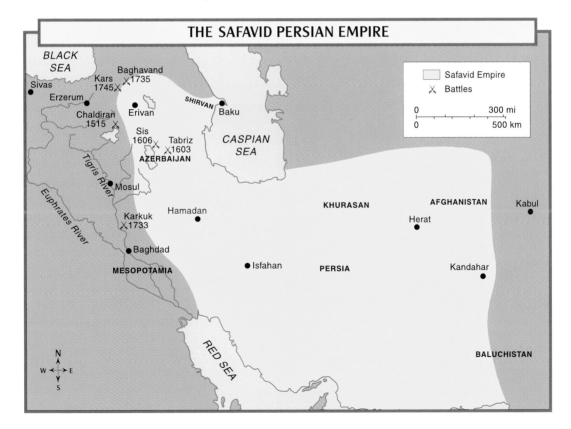

THE SAFAVID PERSIAN EMPIRE

BLACK SEA
Sivas
Erzerum
Kars 1745
Baghavand 1735
Chaldiran 1515
Erivan
SHIRVAN
Baku
Sis 1606
Tabriz 1603
AZERBAIJAN
CASPIAN SEA
Mosul
Hamadan
Karkuk 1733
Baghdad
MESOPOTAMIA
Isfahan
PERSIA
KHURASAN
Herat
AFGHANISTAN
Kabul
Kandahar
BALUCHISTAN
Tigris River
Euphrates River
RED SEA

Safavid Empire
Battles
0   300 mi
0   500 km

N
W E
S

MUGHAL
INDIA

The Mughals ruled India for almost two centuries, from 1526 to 1707. They swept to power in northern India after a series of raids into the region from Afghanistan, their homeland, ended in victory at the Battle of Panipat in 1526. The Mughals, led by Babur, deployed horse-archers and mobile artillery in the battle. The enemy, caught between Mughal gunfire and showers of arrows, collapsed. This firepower was used to crush resistance elsewhere, making the Mughals masters of all India.

Mughal elephants and cavalry from the time of the reign of Akbar, in the late 16th century, pursue a defeated enemy.

Babur was succeeded by his son Humayan in 1530. Humayan made some daring campaigns of conquest but was driven from India and fled to Persia. He began the reconquest of India in 1555 and was succeeded by his son, Akbar. In a series of military campaigns the new Mughal emperor extended the empire from the Hindu Kush Mountains in the north to the center of India.

A reliable army

To control his empire and military forces Akbar appointed ministers. Civil and military officers were given a rank that reflected their pay and duties. A centralized government controlled the empire, supported by tax money collected from landowners. Akbar maintained peace by gaining support from the elite of India's many religious and ethnic groups. These people were permitted to keep their local powers. Religious toleration and Akbar's reliable army helped maintain stability and reduce organized violence.

After Akbar's death in 1605 the throne passed to his son, Jehangir, who fought a series of campaigns against the forces of the state of the Deccan in the south. He was succeeded by his son, Shah Jahan, in 1627. Shah Jahan is perhaps best remembered for building the beautiful Taj Mahal, a tomb to house the mortal remains of his much-loved wife. The new emperor was a capable commander and there was some expansion of the empire. Shah Jahan was finally able to conquer the Deccan. But the finances of the empire began to cause the Mughals problems.

Shah Jahan's son, Aurangzeb, seized the throne in 1659, imprisoned his father, and tried to restore order. Although the empire reached its physical limits under Aurangzeb, his Islamic extremism (he persecuted Hindus) and frictions over tax collection created a weak empire.

Wars of religion

The Moslems of the south of India belonged to the Shiah sect of Islam. Aurangzeb was a Sunni Muslim, the larger sect that considered the Shiah to be heretics. After Aurangzeb conquered the southern Shiah provinces he persecuted the people there. He also attacked the Sikh religion and provoked the Marathas (Hindus in the Deccan) into war.

The Mughal army had by now become a large, slow-moving force composed of huge elephant, artillery, and troop formations. This armed mass became especially vulnerable to the irregular war conducted by the Marathas. Their leader, Shivaji, launched lightning raids on the Mughal's vulnerable supply lines, destroyed crops, and then retreated to strongholds concealed in the mountains of the Deccan region. Aurangzeb, with his empire short of money and many of his troops close to mutiny, was able to hold the empire together—but only just—due to his personal strength as a ruler. However, his successors were by no means as able.

After the death of Aurangzeb in 1707 the dynasty fell into decay and the empire broke into separate kingdoms. Persians and Afghans invaded India, the Marathas became a powerful military force, and new rivals from Europe began to establish colonies along the Indian coast. Dutch, French, Portuguese, and above all, the English began to carve out rival colonies from the ruins of the once-great Mughal Empire.

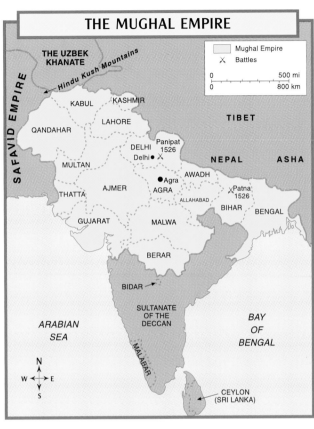

THE MUGHAL EMPIRE

Mughal Empire
X Battles

0   500 mi
0   800 km

The Mughal Empire at the beginning of the 17th century. It would continue to expand until the early years of the following century.

JAPAN'S WARS OF UNIFICATION

In the 15th and early 16th centuries Japan was ruled by a supposedly divine emperor, but an hereditary official called a shogun wielded the real political power. The position of shogun belonged to a single family, the Ashikaga. The Ashikaga had divided the country into many provinces, which they placed under the control of warlords. These warlords frequently fought one another in small wars. Many of them also wanted to become shogun. Their rivalries plunged Japan into a series of civil wars.

By 1550 the shogun, Ashikaga Yoshiteru, had no more authority than the emperor. The Ashikaga had become shogun by marching on the Japanese capital, Kyoto. Other warlords now had ambitions to do the same. In 1560 Imagawa Yoshimoto, who controlled three Japanese provinces, decided to try.

Japanese samurai warriors charge into battle. Like European knights, they lost their battlefield supremacy after gunpowder weapons were introduced into Japan.

A daring commander

Imagawa's route to Kyoto would first take him through Owari province, ruled by the 34-year-old Oda Nobunaga. Oda was a daring commander, however, and took his small army of 2,000 men to confront Imagawa's 25,000 at Dengaku-hazama. The

terrain favored a surprise attack on the rear of Imagawa's army. Oda used this tactic to win the battle. Two of his samurai (aristocratic warriors) killed Imagawa.

Oda now began to prepare for his own march on Kyoto. In 1567 a refugee from a palace revolution in Kyoto arrived in Owari. This refugee, Ashikaga Yoshiaki, could claim to be shogun. Oda decided to use his powerful army to assert this claim. In November 1568 he marched into Kyoto and made Yoshiaki shogun.

Now that Oda controlled the capital, he began to attack warlords who might defy his authority. In 1570 he fought the Battle of Anegawa against Asai Nagamasa, the warlord of Omi province to the north of Kyoto. The two armies charged into the Anegawa River and the fighting took place in the water. Oda won the battle but Asai Nagamasa's army escaped to fight another day. The decisive campaigns occurred in 1573 and 1575. In 1573 Oda deposed Yoshiaki from the shogunate, and gave himself the title of "administrator." Then he attacked Omi and defeated Asai, who committed suicide.

An army of 40,000

In 1575 the warlord of Kai and Shinano provinces, Takeda Katsuyori, struck at Kyoto before Oda could attack him. He got as far as Nagashino castle, which delayed his advance long enough for Oda to assemble an army of nearly 40,000 soldiers. At the Battle of Nagashino, one of the most decisive in Japanese history, Takeda Katsuyori gambled that his well-trained army of 15,000—the best samurai in Japan—could overwhelm Oda's poorer quality force.

Oda had been able to buy gunpowder weapons from Portuguese traders. He had 10,000 soldiers armed with the harquebus. He picked his 3,000 best shots and placed them in three ranks behind a fence of wooden stakes. When Takeda's army

SAMURAI WARFARE

Early Japanese warfare resembled the jousts of medieval knights. The best or most ambitious samurai strode out in front of their respective armies and challenged the best opponents to come out and fight.

Once the two armies charged, battles remained individual struggles. However, several samurai could gang up on a single opponent, provided only one was crossing swords with the outnumbered man at any one time. Tactically, the armies of Europe and the Middle East were much more sophisticated than those of the Japanese.

The arrival of firearms threatened the samurai elite's control of warfare. It allowed the crowds of lowlier soldiers, the ashigaru, to shoot down their social betters, as at the Battle of Nagashino.

One Japanese leader, who had himself risen from the ranks of the ashigaru, took away the firearms of non-samurai. Another imposed a system of gun control that ensured only samurai could carry firearms.

TOYOTOMI HIDEYOSHI

Toyotomi Hideyoshi was born in Owari province, then ruled by the father of Oda Nobunaga. His parents wanted him to be a monk but young Hideyoshi preferred the life of a soldier. He ran away from the temple and became an ordinary soldier. One day, he stole some money and bought a suit of armor, which allowed him to join Oda Nobunaga's army as a samurai.

His rise through the ranks was very fast. During the wars of the 1570s and 1580s Toyotomi was one of Oda's most trusted subordinates. After Oda was killed, Toyotomi Hideyoshi took on the job of seeking revenge for his master's death, which made him Oda's natural successor as political ruler. After ten years of fighting all Japan acknowledged Toyotomi's rule.

In 1592 he began a six-year war to conquer the neighboring peninsula of Korea. The campaign was a failure and the Japanese army evacuated Korea.

charged, the harquebusiers held their fire until their opponents were at close range. Then each rank fired a volley in turn. The constant barrage of harquebus balls, 1,000 every 20 seconds, broke up the Takeda assault. The counterattack swept the Takeda army into history. Although Takeda escaped, he never again posed a threat to Oda.

Murdered by his own general

Oda spent the last years of his life campaigning against the Mori family that controlled the western half of Honshu Island. Oda relied heavily on a samurai named Toyotomi Hideyoshi in the fighting in the west. In 1582 Oda was killed during an attack on his Kyoto home by one of several generals rebelling against his authority.

When Toyotomi heard the news, he made peace with the Mori. He defeated Oda's rebellious generals, then beat Oda's subordinates. The only man opposed to Toyotomi was Tokugawa Ieyasu, the ruler of Imagawa's old lands.

In 1584 the two armies maneuvered for advantage in a campaign that saw their soldiers building defenses rather than fighting. The one battle, at Nagakute on May 17, was a victory for Tokugawa over part of Toyotomi's army. However, the main strength of Toyotomi's army was still more powerful than the Tokugawa army. The two decided to combine to conquer the rest of Japan.

A unified nation

Toyotomi was the senior partner in this alliance. Within three years he had enough strength to invade Kyushu, the southern island of the Japanese group. He assembled a huge army of 250,000 men. The defenders of Kyushu put up a strong resistance at first but surrendered in June 1587. Toyotomi's victory against the defenders of Kyushu marked the beginning of the final stages of the unification of Japan.

After Toyotomi's death in 1598 the struggle to control Japan took two years to begin. Toyotomi's son and heir was only five so a board of nobles took control. This group soon divided between Tokugawa and his opponents. War broke out in the summer of 1600. There was only one major battle, at Sekigahara, on October 21. Thanks to some of his opponent's troops switching sides, Tokugawa won a great victory. He was acclaimed shogun three years later. His descendants ruled Japan until 1868.

Toyotomi Hideyoshi was born into a peasant family but rose through the ranks to become the greatest Japanese warrior of the late 16th century. He brought a previously unknown measure of unity to Japan.

GLOSSARY

battalion A term of French origin developed sometime in the 17th century meaning a unit of some 500 soldiers.

bayonet A knife that a soldier could fix to the end of his musket for hand-to-hand combat. Early examples, known as plug bayonets, were simply rammed into the end of the musket's barrel. Later versions, known as ring bayonets, fitted around the barrel, thereby allowing the soldier to fire.

cartridge A charge of gunpowder and a musket ball wrapped in paper, which greatly increased the speed at which soldiers could reload their muskets.

colunela A word of Spanish origin first used in the late 15th century and early 16th century to describe a unit of infantry commanded by a *cabo de colunela* (chief of column). The word remains in use today in English in the form of colonel, a senior officer.

galleass A type of large galley powered by sails and oars used by several Mediterranean countries in the 16th and 17th centuries. The ships carried soldiers and a number of small guns used to kill enemy soldiers and sailors.

harquebus A type of handheld gunpowder weapon. Developed in the 16th century, it was produced in standardized lengths and calibers.

logistics The supply of all that an army might need to fight effectively This includes food, clothing, weapons, and so on Also the handling of details involved in a military operation

parallel A siege trench, usually dug "parallel" to the walls of an enemy fortification, from where the attacking artillery was in range to smash the fortress's walls.

regiment A military unit of between 500 and 1,000 men, which evolved in the 17th century.

sapper A type of military engineer. The term comes from the term "sap," the narrow, zigzag trench a sapper would dig toward an enemy fortress.

BIBLIOGRAPHY

Note: An asterisk (*) denotes a Young Adult title.

*Brownstone, David, and Franck, Irene. *Timelines of Warfare From 100,000 B.C. to the Present*. Little, Brown and Company, 1994.

Carlton, Charles. *Going to the Wars: The Experience of the British Civil Wars, 1638–1651*. Routledge, 1995.

*Doffleminer, Trina. *Timeline for the Renaissance and Reformation*. Greenleaf, 1997

Dupuy, R. Ernest and Dupuy, Trevor. *The Collins Encyclopedia of Military History*. HaperCollins, 1993

Dupuy, R.E., Johnson, Curt, and Bongard, David L. *The Harper Encyclopedia of Military Biography*. HarperCollins, 1995

*Gaunt, Peter. *The British Wars, 1637–1651*. Routledge, 1997.

*Hall, Bert S. *Weapons and Warfare in Renaissance Europe*. Johns Hopkins University Press, 1997.

Knecht, R.J. *The French Wars of Religion, 1559–1598*. Longman, New York, 1996.

*Lace, William W. *Defeat of the Spanish Armada*. Lucent Books, 1996

Parker, Geoffrey (editor). *The Thirty Years' War*. Routledge, 1997.

Rodgers, W.L. *Naval Warfare Under Oars: 4th to 16th Centuries*. Naval Institute, 1990.

Sire, H.J.A. *The Knights of Malta*. Yale University Press, 1996.

Weigley, Russell F. *The Age of Battles: The Quest for Decisive Warfare from Breitenfeld to Waterloo*. Indiana University Press, 1991.

INDEX

ACKNOWLEDGMENTS

Cover (main picture) AKG Photo, London (inset), Peter Newark's Military Pictures; page 1 Peter Newark's Military Pictures; page 5 AKG Photo, London; page 6 Peter Newark's Military Pictures; page 9 AKG Photo, London; page 10 AKG Photo, London; page 13 AKG Photo, London/Joseph Martin; page 14 Peter Newark's Military Pictures; page 15 Peter Newark's Military Pictures; page 17 AKG Photo, London; page 18 Peter Newark's Military Pictures; page 19 Peter Newark's Military Pictures; page 20 AKG Photo, London; page 22 AKG Photo, London; page 24 Hulton Getty Collection; page 25 AKG Photo, London; page 27 Peter Newark's Military Pictures; page 28 Peter Newark's Historical Pictures; page 29 Peter Newark's Historical Pictures, page 31 Peter Newark's Military Pictures; page 32 AKG Photo, London; page 34 Peter Newark's Military Pictures; page 35 Peter Newark's Military Pictures; page 36 AKG Photo, London; page 38 Peter Newark's Military Pictures; page 39 AKG Photo, London; page 40 Peter Newark's Military Pictures; page 41 AKG Photo, London; page 42 Peter Newark's Military Pictures; page 43 Peter Newark's Military Pictures; page 44 Peter Newark's Military Pictures; page 47 Peter Newark's Military Pictures; page 49 Peter Newark's Military Pictures; page 50 Peter Newark's Military Pictures; page 51 Peter Newark's Military Pictures; page 53 Peter Newark's Military Pictures; page 55 Peter Newark's Military Pictures; page 56 Peter Newark's Military Pictures; page 58 Peter Newark's Military Pictures; page 59 AKG Photo, London; page 60 AKG Photo, London; page 61 Peter Newark's Historical Pictures; page 62 Peter Newark's Military Pictures; page 65 AKG Photo/Eric Lessing; page 66 AKG Photo, London; page 67 AKG Photo, London; page 68 Peter Newark's Military Pictures; page 70 Mary Evans Picture Library; page 72 AKG Photo, London; page 74 Peter Newark's Military Pictures; page 77 Peter Newark's Military Pictures.